The *Sky Rider* had been torn apart. Rooms and corridors ended a few feet away. Jagged walls opened onto empty space. Walkways and floors led into nowhere. Twisted girders hung suspended over a yawning abyss and great chunks of her hull slowly revolved, hurtling outward and onward into the universe. Her wreckage stretched for miles. And among it floated the bodies of people, dead and drifting in a graveyard of stars.

With a choked cry Glyn turned away. He went running, stumbling, back along the corridor. He wanted to scream in the loneliness. And no one could help him.

"Lawrence deftly threads her crackling characterizations through a highly charged plot that is set against the stark but vividly depicted backdrop of space.... Spielberg could have fun with this one."
—ALA *Booklist*

"A fascinating adventure."
—*School Library Journal*

"Spine-chilling and exciting reading."
—*The Horn Book*

LOUISE LAWRENCE

CALLING
B FOR BUTTERFLY

HarperKeypoint
An Imprint of HarperCollinsPublishers

Library of Congress Cataloging-in-Publication Data
Lawrence, Louise, 1943–
  Calling B for Butterfly.

  Summary: Four teenagers must fend for
themselves and two babies when the space liner
on which they are traveling is destroyed by an asteroid.
  [1. Science fiction] I. Title.
PZ7.L4367Ca 1982   [Fic]   81-48648
ISBN 0-06-023749-X
ISBN 0-06-023750-3 (lib. bdg.)
ISBN 0-06-447036-9 (pbk.)

Harper Keypoint is an imprint of Harper Trophy,
a division of HarperCollins Publishers.
First Harper Keypoint edition, 1988.

To KEN and MARGO
in gratitude

1

It was a terrible, violent place, fabulous and fascinating. Crimson, vermillion, ochre yellow and rusty brown, the clouds swirled—ethane, methane and phosphine, making shifting whirlpools of color in a raging hydrogen atmosphere. White spots formed and fled in the hurricane winds, erupting like pustules a thousand miles wide, and the bolt lightning flashed. Red and gold in the black sky beyond, the aurorae hung in delicate shimmering veils of light and a fine dusty ring curved away into space. To that vision of beauty and terror Joe had given the best years of his life.

With an effort he turned his back on Jupiter. In the lurid light he crossed the domed observatory. It was quiet between shifts. Frobisher was pruning the begonias, working his way from pot to pot among empty desks and meteorological machinery. Joe nodded a greeting and went to join Anton at the computer controls. Here, on the opposite side of the room, the windows gave him a different view—basalt and stars and a sheen of black ice. Gloomy and hostile, the rugged surface of Ganymede stretched out before him, dark and dead, stark rocks and craters, gaping fissures and tracts of flat featureless terrain. Here there was nothing beautiful. It was a frozen world, airless and lifeless. Nothing moved in the desolate landscape. Nothing survived but a handful of men.

But something moved among the stars.

In the utter blackness, out beyond the orbit of Callisto, Joe noticed two tiny pinpoints of light and adjusted the telescanner. Clear and sharp on the video screen, the starliners came into focus—the *Star Flight* and the *Pegasus*—heading out into the galaxy with their cargo of emigrants. Tiny life ferries clung like limpets to their sides. Joe fed time and position into the computer data bank. White numbers filled a flickering screen. It was a routine traffic check, and the starliners were right on schedule.

Frobisher peered over his shoulder.

"Where's the *Sky Rider?*"

"She'll be a few weeks behind," Joe told him.

"A delayed departure," said Anton. "Something wrong with her deflector shields."

"How come I wasn't informed?" Frobisher asked.

"It hardly seemed relevant, sir," Joe said.

Frobisher frowned.

His white shaggy eyebrows drew together in an expression of annoyance. As Base Controller he expected to be informed of all things, however irrelevant. But his anger changed direction. The survey ship came in to land, flying fast and low above the sprawl of buildings. The rooms shook, and out on the runway the ground crew ducked and ran for cover.

"Which idiot is flying that ship?" Frobisher snapped.

"J. P. Mackenzie," Anton said.

"Do I know him?"

"He arrived last week on the cargo tug."

Frobisher nodded grimly.

"Have him report to my office," Frobisher said.

It was 1315 hours.

There was a feeling in the air—a kind of imminence.

3

Departure time was fifteen minutes away.

"Go and watch, can I?" Glyn asked.

The chief steward straightened his back.

"Are you on the passenger list?"

"No," said Glyn.

"In that case," said the chief steward, "you're here to work."

Glyn scowled.

It was not work, it was donkey work, and already he was sick of it. He had been keen enough when he had applied for the post of steward aboard the *Sky Rider*. He would have done anything to get away from home, from his mother's temper and his father's drunkenness. But he had not imagined it would be like this—mindless servitude in the General Supplies Department and six weeks' delay. All he did was shift stock—hump damned great boxes of vitamin orange and powdered egg, cartons of dried meat cubes and dehydrated potatoes. He was not even allowed to use the motorized trailers without supervision. But once, as a special treat, he had been told to take the vacuum polisher and clean the corridor. It was the size of a street and had taken him three days. Now he piled linen into the laundry cart, one week's supply of spare sheets for families with young children—and the ship was about to take off.

It was 1325 hours.

If he were quick he could just make it.

He clipped the cabin list to the handle and heaved the cart around. The doors opened automatically, but the wheels slued and stuck, each one going in a different direction. Glyn swore quietly and kicked at them. A combination of brute force and annoyance got the contraption out into the corridor. It was empty, as always, but now the pale-green linoleum he had polished was dull and dusty, scuffed by people's feet—and the walls he had washed shone in the light and showed the smears of childish fingerprints. The trundle of the cart and Glyn's footsteps sounded loud as a grievance.

He had no way of knowing when it happened. The takeoff was soundless. Inch by inch the *Sky Rider* edged away from the orbiting space station and slowly gathered momentum. There was no vibration from her drive units. There was no sensation of speed. Unaffected, Glyn turned the corner into the main thoroughfare and, for the first time since he had arrived on board, he encountered the general public—a stream of passengers, all wanting to go where he wanted to go, thronging toward the elevators and the observation platform. They impeded his progress. Wearing his maroon uniform, he was obliged to stop and give them directions, and when he finally got there he was too late—the Earth had dwindled in size,

5

and the great revolving wheel of the space station with its myriad lights looked no bigger than a tiny toy. He had missed the moment. And all around him were bright eyes and excited voices, the flushed faces of people who thrilled with an experience he had failed to share. It was not disappointment Glyn felt—it was the desire to run the cart into the nearest pair of legs.

"Get out of the way!" Glyn said angrily.

The girl rounded on him.

She wore a tight scarlet sweater and a sour expression.

"Who do you think you're talking to?" she asked.

The stars stayed still. Only Earth moved, brilliant blue, falling backward in space. And the moon, pale as a face, floated past the window. Ann watched them—twin worlds diminishing into a black infinity. She would never see them again.

"It's so sad."

Her father put his arm around her shoulder.

"It's the finality, my darling."

"It reminds me of Mummy," Ann said.

The moon reminded her.

A cold crematorium on a January day.

"We have to forget," her father said firmly.

But it was not her mother's death that troubled Ann, the house full of absence and memories and the brass plaque beneath a rosebush—it was a kind of fear. She glanced around. Everywhere there were people—a chaos of people all congregated together on the observation platform to watch the departure, unknown faces and unfamiliar voices, each one of them a stranger. It was the people who made Ann afraid—the whimpering child and the girl in the scarlet sweater, the tall boy with glasses and the young starship steward in his maroon uniform who pushed a laundry cart. Soon she would have to meet them, mix with them, in the communal halls and the dining rooms. And tomorrow she would have to start school.

Nerves crawled in her stomach.

Her socks slipped around her ankles.

She was afraid of everything.

"You're not sorry we came, are you?" her father asked.

"No," said Ann.

But she was.

Beyond the railed-off gantry was a great drop going hideous and sheer in a pool of light all the way down to the floor below. It made her feel sick. She turned to gaze back through the window, but she could still feel it behind her— the great ship stretching away. It was too vast, too huge—a mile-long city traveling through space, a warren of rooms and corridors and living quarters, and this hall now, like a great cathedral, with herself standing small inside it staring out at a different vastness. The stars stayed still—pin-pricks of gold among lonely galaxies where human people had never been. It was beautiful and awful. She was afraid of that too—the black endless distances between the stars.

"Shall we go back to the cabin?" Ann asked.

Her father looked at her.

"Wouldn't you rather visit the recreation rooms?"

"They're sure to be crowded," Ann said.

"Then how about the leisure garden?"

"We don't know where it is."

"We can find out," her father told her.

Ann gripped the handrail.

She did not want to go anywhere—but neither did she want to stay on her own. Alone, the terror took over. She needed her father to make her feel safe. She hurriedly pulled up her socks. "Wait for me, Daddy!" Hard metal slammed into her thigh. A wheel crushed her foot. The young steward glowered at her. She was fair-haired and colorless in her beige traveling suit—jittery as a moth in the harsh light. She bit her lip and her eyes glimmered with tears.

Glyn backed the cart.

"Look where you're going!" he said rudely.

"We're very sorry," Ann's father said.

They had been a month late leaving Earth. They had been cooped up for two weeks in the space station. It had all been very boring. And it was even more boring on board the *Sky Rider*. Not that Sonja had expected it to be anything else. She saw nothing to marvel at—no glory in the infinite stars. She was locked away in the dour blackness of her own mood. She had never wanted to come—never wanted to leave the life in London, the plush restaurants and high-fashion shops, the rock groups and disco dances, the big house in the suburbs and her circle of friends. But the family unit had to remain intact. Sandwiched between her elder and younger brother, and not yet sixteen, Sonja had had no choice.

"I want to hear no more about it," said her mother.

And the departure was irreversible.

It sealed the end of everything.

Bitter and resenting, Sonja began the journey—nine months across space to the colony on Omega Five, where her father would be taking up some obscure diplomatic position. It was an archaic policy, like the British in India after the death of Queen Victoria trying to hold on to their empire of rubber plantations and polo ponies. Only now it was a load of emigrants wanting political independence, land clearance and mineral rights, and maintaining good interplanetary relations.

Sonja hated the stars.

She turned her back on them, leaned against the windowsill and narrowed her eyes against the light. The walkway that circled the vast observation hall was crowded with people. She could hear the boom of her mother's voice over by the elevators, loud and patronizing—jollying along some unfortunate woman with a bawling infant and a whimpering child. Her mother's favorite occupation was organizing other people's lives. But a fair-haired girl in an awful beige jersey suit blocked Sonja's view. She was clutching the handrail, limping and sniveling, and a man put an arm around her shoulder. Her father, Sonja supposed. Farther along the gantry her own father stood with Jeffrey and Simon, watching the world slip away. And perhaps, if she had not been so insufferably crushing, the steward with the laundry cart might have stayed and talked to her. Sonja toyed with her neck chain. Beaten gold against the background of her scarlet sweater, a desanctified Saint Christopher hid his face against her breast. She was not used to insignificance.

She stole a look at the boy standing next to her. He was tall and studious in his steel-rimmed glasses. His chin rested on his hand as he stared outward—his faraway gaze noticing no one. It was a thoughtful pose, almost poetic—and his face was gentle, not brash. A couple of months ago she would not have looked twice at him. Now she wondered who he was and where he came from. She was about to ask when someone dragged at her arm. There was an inane grin on Jeffrey's face.

"Isn't it spectacular?" Jeffrey said.

"I hadn't noticed," Sonja said sourly.

"Dad reckons we're doing about two hundred miles a second," Jeffrey gabbled. "He reckons we'll catch up with the *Star Flight* and the *Pegasus* before we reach Uranus. I can't wait to leave the solar system and enter warp drive. You know the reason why we can't go straight into warp drive? It's because—"

"Why don't you warp off!" Sonja told him.

The *Sky Rider* was building up speed. Two hundred miles a second, the small boy had said. But already it was more than that—velocity increasing and increasing across the solar system. She would catch up with her sister ships long before they entered interstellar space. Days meant nothing to the *Sky Rider*. She defied time. Once into warp drive she could reduce weeks into seconds, years into weeks—crossing through barriers of curving light to reemerge among new worlds floating around a different sun.

A cosmic butterfly.

Matthew thought of it.

There was nothing fragile about the *Sky*

11

Rider. She was a mile-long metal hulk hurtling through space, wingless and ungainly. She could ram a path clear through the asteroid belt with her great deflector shields. Yet the analogy remained—the sheen of her walls in the dusty light and the compound eyes of her computers. And Earth faded like a bright-blue flower she had once fed upon, and the moon swept past her—fungoid white, unappetizing and ignored. People too contained the allusion—the girl with nectar hair in her quiet mothy colors, nervous and fluttering with nowhere to settle, there and now gone. Now, in her place, was a different girl, uncomfortably close—the bold flash of her scarlet sweater reflecting on the rim of his glasses. He heard the angry tone of her voice and kept his back to her, fixed his eyes on the stars.

Megrez, Alioth, Merak and Phad. The names of stars were strange and beautiful.

Beautiful as the butterflies Matthew studied.

Still at high school, he was too young to be classed as an expert, but he was more than an amateur. His parents were botanists and he had been born and bred among the classifications of flora and fauna and the identification of species. His sister kept dung beetles in an old aquarium, became a zoologist and married one, and Matthew had taken up lepidoptery at the age of seven. Apart from his father, who dealt with the diseases of cereal crops, they were all pursuing obsolete occupations. On Earth all species were known and catalogued, and the natural environment had almost disappeared. The chalk-hill blue and the swallowtail were gone out of Europe now. The Amazon green, the New Guinea bird wing and the scarlet fritillary were gone from the world. Crimson and orange, gaudy yellow and electric blue—the butterflies were preserved—their gorgeous wings protected by glass, their bodies pinned on boards in cold museums.

But there were butterflies on Omega Five. Unknown, unnamed, in an unspoiled world, they waited to be discovered. With the rest of his family, Matthew was going there on a three-year grant along with a traveling buggy, research equipment and unlimited supplies of film. Wet woods and mountains, swamps and tundra, birds, beasts and flowers—a whole planet would be his to explore. Omegan butterflies flew in clouds through his brain.

"I suppose you wanted to come?"

A girl's voice posed the question.

And waited for an answer.

Matthew looked around to see who she was talking to. She was apparently talking to him, but he did not know her. She made him feel awkward. He took off his glasses, wiped them on the corner of his jacket. She became blurred then—a scarlet girl amid a misty moving background of people and light.

"I supposed you wanted to come on this trip," she repeated.

"Didn't you?" Matthew asked her.

"No," she said. "My mother forced me."

Matthew replaced his glasses.

She looked petulant and unsmiling.

He did not particularly want to know her.

"Please excuse me," Matthew said. "I have to find my sister. I promised to baby-sit."

2

Matthew knew the rules.

It was unlawful to bring any unauthorized livestock aboard an interplanetary vessel. But the small brown scraps of life dwelled in a plastic container in his locker and lay like guilt on his mind. His conscience drove him. He wrestled with it for weeks and finally gave up. In the early Monday afternoon he skipped school and headed back toward the cabin. There was no one about— there never was at that time of day. They were all away in other parts of the ship: his mother and father in the bio labs, his sister and her husband in the microfilm library and baby Eleanor in the starship nursery. Silent and unwitnessed, Matthew went to expiate his crime.

The long corridors were quiet and empty. His shoes squeaked on the linoleum and the rattle of loose change in his pocket broke the silence. The sound of his own presence unnerved him. He stopped to listen.

Faintly, far away, he heard music playing and the soft humming of a motorized trailer. He had forgotten it was laundry day. He started to run, past closed doors set in pale-green walls, confusing and featureless. B30, B32—even after five weeks he still needed to check the numbers—B34, B36. Matthew pressed the button and entered the cabin, and the door slid shut behind him with a quiet thud.

He was quite safe.

The steward had already been.

A pile of clean sheets stood on the small center table and the linen bin was empty. Matthew picked his way across a floor that was strewn with natural history magazines, dropped pages of cramped handwriting, Eleanor's building bricks and a bell rattle, and entered the tiny cubicle that posed as a bedroom. Moths sang in the dark—and below the tapes that contained their music he found the container, clear plastic with breathing holes. Gently Matthew opened it. They looked dark and dead on their white bed of cotton wool—like broken bits of winter sticks that would never shoot or take root. But Matthew knew what lived and formed inside them—what winged beauty would hatch from those drab cocoons.

"Thou shalt not kill," the commandment said.

There was an incinerator in the wall.

Matthew lifted the lid.

But he could not do it.

Mars went by—red as a blood orange. And then there was nothing—nothing but time and her own fear. Ann suffered it—long hours of every day when she was separated from her father. She could put names to the faces now, but it was no easier. She still did not know them. Miss Mousie, the teachers called her. Drip, said the girls when she failed to catch the basketball. She stayed on the outside and was never one of them, and each day contained a different dread.

On Monday afternoons it was gymnastics.

And sometimes Ann could make it happen deliberately. She applied a pressure to the bone inside her nose and released it in a warm red trickle. It did not always work. But it worked that particular Monday afternoon during the preceding arithmetic lesson. Bright drops of blood fell on a paper tissue. She tried to stem the flow but it was too much. She started to feel queer. Her head swam, and mathematical symbols floated on a black background. She pushed back her chair and one by one the girls turned to look at her.

"Please, Miss—Ann Trethowen has a nose-bleed," someone said.

"Oh dear," said the teacher.

The blood protected Ann.

It made them kind and concerned.

She did not need to be afraid.

"You'd better go to the Health Center," the teacher said.

There were doctors at the Health Center. Ann did not want to go there, but she left the classroom gladly. A girl came with her and put an arm around her shoulders. She offered to go and find Ann's father—but he was at the agricultural classes and for once she did not want him. She would be all right on her own, she said. It was only a nosebleed. When the girl returned to lessons Ann went back to her cabin.

A long way ahead of her someone was running, and a long way behind her came the sound of a motorized trailer. And somewhere she heard music. But the door shut it out. In the stillness and silence without people she lay on her bunk— and the walls were around her, a cubicle room, small and safe like a white womb. The nosebleed stopped but she did not move. She stayed where she was with the memories of Earth in her mind— a village street under sunlight, the apple-faced lady who kept the post office and the green lanes of Devon where she used to walk.

Earth was too far behind, an unbridgeable distance. The radio stations with their nonstop pop music no longer reached them and the television programs were all recorded. Nobody knew who topped the charts anymore. Nobody cared except Sonja and the group of girls she went about with. There was nothing new on board the *Sky Rider*. Night after night at the under-eighteens' club the disc jockey played the same old sounds. The Coke lost its fizz and the flashing red-green dancing lights never changed their sequence. It was all familiar now, as familiar as the faces of boys whom Sonja met and lost interest in. But Simon moved in a different age group—higher education and heavy rock. And someone had lent him a cassette by the Galaxy Hunters that Sonja had never heard before.

That afternoon, when everyone was out and the apartments were empty, Sonja did not attend lessons. She listened to the music instead and polished her toenails. With the volume on high she stayed mindless inside it, lost in the sweet-sugar-pink-pearldrop scent and the wailing thumping sound. It was like a drug. It obliterated thought and took her over. The Galaxy Hunters—their electric music blasted away her boredom. Beyond them nothing else mattered. They

19

seemed to contain everything—poetry, religion, politics, life itself. It was as if Sonja was actually living through them, her mind and emotion caught by the heavy music and transcending everyday existence. Wild voices took her away.

> *Think you can leave it behind, babe—*
> *go out of the world—*
> *kill the man with the stars in his eyes?*
> *He's got the time, babe—*
> *and you've got the distance to run.*
> *He can shoot down the sky*
> *with his eyes. . . .*

Sonja listened. Words with their obscure meanings formed a series of changing images that dissolved in the light before she could take them in, and the sound gripped her guts like a pain. She wanted to shed her body of flesh and blood and turn into music, merge with the sound like a kind of love.

> *With me there's no loneliness, lady—*
> *just endless flight—*
> *metal angels on the star roads—*
> *wings among the light.*

Sonja's head swayed to the rhythm. Nail polish dripped from the end of her brush.

Glyn was collecting dirty bed linen and replacing it with clean. It was part of the service—

a slow stop-start process, opening closed cabin doors and emptying linen bins. The motorized trailer was no consolation. Once the first thrill of learning to drive it had worn off, the monotony had set in—day after day of never-varying routine, sheets and towels and pillowcases. He knew the allocations by heart now. He knew every corridor, every cabin, every name on the delivery list. He knew who occupied every cramped windowless apartment on board the *Sky Rider*. But he seldom saw them.

During daylight hours the cabin area was usually deserted. Abandoned in the light, the long corridors were echoing and lonely. The people were gone to other parts of the ship—the schools and lecture halls, canteens, gardens and swimming pools, recreation rooms, sports halls or television lounges, the day nursery, the libraries, laboratories, handicraft clubs or government training plans. On board the *Sky Rider* there was no time for boredom or idleness. But Glyn had turned down his chances at college for the lure of high wages—and he wondered how long it would be before he went mad.

A month of Sundays?

A month of Mondays?

Or was it six weeks?

Mars had gone by and the ship had entered the asteroid belt, but Glyn had lost track of time. It was hard to distinguish one day from the next—

21

they were all the same, purr of the trailer down empty corridors.

But that afternoon he heard someone running and saw a girl turn down a side corridor. He even heard music. It was nothing to do with him, but at least he was not alone. He was working his way through B deck—cabin after cabin, small and personalized with plastic-framed photographs, kids' toys and passengers' belongings. A thieves' paradise. Glyn resisted the diamond dress ring that lay on a table—but he tried on the gloves. They were white and smooth, spotless as a soap advertisement. He realized he would never make a starship captain, but maybe one day he would serve cocktails of an evening in one of the glittering bars. He draped a towel over his arm and studied himself in the mirror.

"How d'you want it, missis? Slopped or stirred?"

His reflection stared back at him.

"Try speaking proper," Glyn advised himself. He cleared his throat. His Welsh accent changed into mincing English.

"One tomato juice, modom, with a dash of Worcestershire."

And the lights flickered.

3

The lights flickered. There was no other warning. Like a bolt out of space the sound struck—boomed through the hollow hull, reverberated like thunder and fled in a wave of shock. An impact of rock against metal walls, crushing, tearing, like a car in a breaker's yard, but a thousand times louder, a thousand times more swift. The *Sky Rider* shuddered and lurched. Her rooms keeled at crazy angles. Contents spilled from her cupboards and crashed to the floor as she listed and righted herself. Her circuits were severed and the lights went out. In the nightmare dark her girders groaned and settled. And then there was silence.

23

Absolute silence.

Absolute dark.

It was deaf and blind—sensory deprivation where minds lost a grip on themselves and the terror began. Sonja screamed. Some hideous happening she did not know about had killed the music and pitched her to the floor. There was a pain in her arm, and broken pieces of cassette recorder cut at her knees like unseen glass. She tried to brush them away, but her hands grew sticky. There was blood on her leg, blood on the carpet. She could feel it, touch it, and the scent of spilled nail polish was cloying and sweet. Stripped of her sight she made no connection. Stunned by the darkness, she screamed again, groped for the table and pulled herself up. She had only one thought. She had to get out of there.

Matthew clung to the sink unit, listened and waited. The ship stayed still. Nothing moved, nothing sounded—only the darkness that battered his eyes—only his breath in the silence and the thud of his heart. It was as if, for a moment, he had ceased to exist and then he began again, but he was not the same anymore. Everything that had given him identity was gone. Time, light and people were swept away and he was alone— alone and sightless, like a gone-wrong computer with the thoughts all scrambled up in his mind. The paralyzing seconds ticked away, merging fear into instinct that drove him into action. He had to do something, now, in the black growing urgency to save himself.

He felt on the floor for his glasses.

Ann lay still. After the last creak of sound and her heart's wild hammering had ended there was only the darkness. It settled around her, warm and enveloping, and she did not question it. It was like the night, when all the ship was quiet and sleeping and the fears of the day were over. She welcomed it. Perhaps she even loved it. The kind blind silence made her feel safe and strong. No one could see her and she could hear and see no one—no intimidating eyes, no voices crushing and sarcastic making her feel useless and small. There was only herself in the black beautiful freedom, knowing that something had happened, not knowing what but glad that it had. She hoped it would go on, just as it was, dark without light. And her childlike trust allowed no conception of final abandonment. She smiled in the safety of her solitude. Soon her father would come and there was nothing to worry about.

Glyn forgot ambition. He scrambled to his feet. The table had cracked and broken under his weight but he could not see it. The darkness was a wall against his eyes, obliterating everything, and the silence boomed in his ears. He had lost all sense of direction, all conception of shape and form. In the black brutal aftermath of the experience, the godawful fear lay inside him. This was no space-suit drill. This was for real. They had been rammed by an asteroid.

"Don't talk stupid," Glyn muttered.

The *Sky Rider* had deflector shields, he knew that. They had been defective and had had to be repaired, which was why they were late. But what had been defective once could become defective again. The fear remained. Some asteroids were hundreds of miles wide, galactic bulldozers big as worlds. They could crush her hull like a grape.

"Don't think of it," he advised himself.

But the thought stayed, preyed, persisted like knowledge.

He had to get out of there.

He had to reach the nearest life ferry.

"Don't panic, boyo!"

It was not quite dark. Over on the wall was an illuminated panel, a small square similar to a fire alarm sign. Words glowed in the glass, red as blood and terrible in meaning. EMERGENCY, they said. BREAK GLASS TO RELEASE DOOR. Glyn stared at them. He knew about the *Sky Rider*.

She contained automatic safety devices. In event of an accident her doors hermetically sealed themselves. The fear renewed itself and became confirmed. He started to pray.

"Our Father, who art in heaven—where's the blasted space suits kept?"

The words glowed red.

They meant nothing to Sonja.

In the shut cabin she screamed and pummeled the door that would not open. She beat with her fists and clawed at it. Desperate and futile, her fingers pried at the crack, trying to force a way out. And still it would not open. Her screams changed to a shrill crying, disjointed and inhuman, and her terror gave way to despair. She would die there, alone in the dark with no one to help her. Die in the dragged-out seconds long as hours where nothing could relieve the terrible awareness of herself—the fear and the loneliness and the blood. She sank to the floor and wept.

Matthew widened his search in the debris and the dark. Dried crackers and a baby bottle had fallen to the floor and a box of milk powder had spilled its contents. He could feel it—soft as dust beneath his fingers. He touched soft sounds—the crackle of cellophane and the jingle of bells on Eleanor's rattle. Then his hand closed thankfully over the steel frames of his glasses and his touch told him the lenses were intact.

Vision in darkness.

It was not the glasses that restored his sight.

Silently, eerily, the emergency lighting switched itself on, triggered by a minute drop in temperature. Strip lights in the ceiling over him slowly brightened, the dull yellow of solar batteries dispelling the fear, restoring all things to normal. He was himself again—seeing, perceiving, thinking rational thoughts. This was the *Sky Rider*, a galactic starliner. She was structurally invincible, and the odds against a major accident in space were a million to one. But the clock had stopped at 15:15 and the rooms were full of wreckage, and beside the door was an illuminated panel. Matthew stared at it. The words shone crimson as balefire and the meaning burned in his mind.

The suit was pale silver, insulated metallic fabric that inflated automatically into a grotesque human shape. Recorded instructions told Glyn what to do. He climbed inside and the nasal voice repeated and repeated each step of the procedure until he had it right. He was sealed in and the oxygen cylinder was hard against his back. He wore it like a knapsack, connected the tube and switched on. Cool gas brushed his face like a breath and the twin dials on his wrist showed dual green. The impersonal voice droned on inside the helmet.

"You are all systems go. All systems go. Repeat—you are all systems go."

And the tape ended abruptly with a click.

Glyn was left standing, alone in the silence of his mind, with twenty minutes left to live. Cold sweat beaded his skin. His heart banged in his rib cage and his breath made a small mist on the plastic visor, which instantly faded. He raised his fist to smash the glass and release the door, but he could not do it. He was afraid. Afraid of what was outside—a black vacuum where blood boiled and nothing survived.

"You listening, God?" Glyn asked.

But only the hiss of the air supply answered him.

"It's your decision, boyo," Glyn told himself.

It was not blood. It was nail polish. Sonja could see it in the light, dried on her legs like a pink skin. Nail polish and a power failure—she had had hysterics for no reason. Her stupidity made her angry. All that emotion—for nothing! She got to her feet, blew her nose on a handful of colored tissues and studied her face in the mirror. Black mascara streaked her cheeks and her hair was a mess. She despised herself. A couple of minutes of noise and darkness and she had screamed like a small child. People did not

29

die on board the *Sky Rider* and accidents did not happen in space, not these days. But behind her was the apartment full of fallen broken things, the yellow wrongness of the light and the closed outer door. Beside it was a sign, glowing red, words reversed and unreadable. Sonja turned.

EMERGENCY, they said.

BREAK GLASS TO RELEASE DOOR.

And finally she understood.

The light destroyed the sanctuary of the darkness. Sickly and yellow it filled the cabin, throwing long shadows where none had been before, making all things look strange and unfamiliar. Ann could no longer deceive herself. Something was wrong. The clock had stopped, digital time at 15:15 gone terrifyingly still—and the hiss of the air conditioning was missing. Unbearable silence. She sat on the edge of her bunk and chewed her fingernails. It was not beautiful anymore. The silence was too intense, and there was a feeling of lateness in the air—like the scent of autumn on July evenings, a hint of mist, of coming cold, dewfall and death. It was almost an animal sensing. Anxiety grew in the pit of her stomach. Her mind pitched toward panic. She waited for her father to come and find her.

For the last time Matthew stared around the apartment. He could take nothing with him, only the memory. Contents of rooms in a gloomy light—the discarded files of his father's research and his mother's life, the dropped toys of a child, the photograph of his sister's wedding day—it all seemed out of place here. This was only a transition place between two worlds, filled with the traces of a brief stay. There was nothing he wanted to keep. But on the floor by the incinerator he noticed the plastic container. Unknowing, unheeding, the butterflies slept in their brown cocoons, secret companions on a voyage to a star. His silver-gloved hand closed over them. He secured them inside his suit and turned to go.

Instinct and survival.

In nature there was no room for indecision.

The glass smashed soundlessly beneath the spike heel of his sister's shoe, and slowly and soundlessly the outer door started to open. He expected to hear the shriek of escaping air, but enclosed in the space suit he could hear nothing—just the hiss of breath and oxygen. And nothing moved, no hurtling of things toward the crack sucked by the vacuum outside—just himself anchored in the stillness and the slowly opening door. A threshold to the future—Matthew stood on the edge of it. And the dials on his wrist showed dual green, indicating that the atmosphere remained breathable. There was no need for a space suit. But he had to risk death to make sure. For a moment he hesitated, then like a kind

31

of test he released the suction seal, lifted the face visor and took a deep breath.

Out into the lonely corridor Matthew stepped.

Red arrows flashed the way to the life ferry.

And a long way ahead of him someone was walking.

4

There was writing on the wall—illuminated signs saying LIFE FERRY B—and the arrows flashed, bright red and glassy, indicating the way. Down the dimly lit corridors Glyn and Matthew walked together. They did not know each other, but it was more than a brief hello that bound them. Each for the other ended the fear and the isolation, and there were no more appalling singular decisions to make. The closed entrance to the life ferry was just a small problem solved by common agreement. There was no mental and emotional agony involved in pressing the button—no questioning. The air lock opened and let them in, but the inner door stayed closed against them and through the dark square of glass they could see nothing. The belly of the ship was black and dead. Glyn felt the panic start again.

"There's no one here!"

Matthew read the written instructions.

" 'In vacuum conditions press red button to close outer door.' That doesn't apply to us. 'Depress switch marked A.P.' Nor does that. 'Check Air Pressure gauge.' Yes. 'When pointer enters green area, indicating normal, a green light will show above inner door.' That's there. 'When light shows green, press button to open inner door. CAUTION—IT IS DANGEROUS TO OPEN INNER DOOR WHEN LIGHT SHOWS RED.' But as it's green," said Matthew, "all we need do is open it."

"But there's no one in there, boyo!" Glyn repeated.

"There will be in a minute," Matthew said.

Triggered by the opening of the door, the ferry ship blazed into life. A flood of white light almost blinded them, brilliant as day and reflecting on the curved walls and sterile surfaces. Matthew narrowed his eyes. The ship was sleek and streamlined, pristine and beautiful, big as a jet plane back on Earth with her double rows of silver seats and a gangway down the middle. She could seat two hundred people and carry them to safety.

But now there was no one aboard her. She waited, primed and empty, to fulfill her purpose.

"We must be the first to arrive," Matthew said.

"So what do we do?" Glyn asked.

There was nothing they could do, only take off their space suits and wait. The waiting was long and hard. An unset clock on the cabin wall was hours wrong and needed adjusting. Its slow digital clicks grated on Glyn's nerves. The lights hummed. Heat and air shimmered above the vents. Live circuits ticked like time, and again and again Matthew checked his watch. Twenty minutes passed.

"We could have come to the wrong place," Glyn said.

" 'In event of an accident go to your nearest life ferry,' " Matthew quoted.

"You heard the alarm bell, did you?" Glyn asked him.

"No."

"Nor did I. So what are we doing here?"

"You know as well as I do," Matthew said.

"Yes," said Glyn. "But where's the rest of 'em?"

"Maybe there *is* no one else."

"Don't talk stupid!" Glyn's fear was covered by anger. "There's twelve hundred people on board the *Sky Rider*! One thousand passengers

and two hundred crew! They can't all have . . .
I mean . . . it's hardly likely. There's bound to
be someone!"

His voice trailed away.

He conveyed what he thought by what he
did not say.

Matthew understood. You could not pro-
nounce that kind of thing. Put into words, it became a death sentence, like a hideous fact he was
not prepared to face. He preferred to count the
odds against it—the likelihood of its not happening. Twelve hundred people did not die in a few
split seconds of time. There was bound to be
someone.

"It stands to reason," Glyn said.

He was quite right.

Minutes later footsteps sounded in the corridor outside, and one more space-suited figure
found its way to Life Ferry B. Fully helmeted,
Sonja stood in the doorway—faceless, sexless and
vaguely human in shape. Light shone on her visor. Silver metallic arms gesticulated wildly. The
boys had hoped she was a responsible adult, but
her muffled voice was shrill and female and she
had left her vanity case behind.

Ann sat and waited.

She was sick and afraid and she felt in her
stomach a dull hopelessness that was worse than
grief. She could not cry because of it. If she cried

it would mean she believed her father would never come, and she could not believe that. Soon he would come for her, she told herself, and clung to the thought. She would wait for him forever if she had to. But the apartment was growing cold, although perhaps she only imagined it. And perhaps she only imagined the light was beginning to fade. It was not a perceptible change. If it happened at all it happened gradually, like frost at nightfall, a slow cooling of the air and the shadows deepening. Fetus-shaped, she huddled beneath the blankets. Now and then she thought of leaving, but she did not know where to go, and alone, without her father, her life did not mean very much. Soon he would come for her. Soon he was bound to come.

Matthew helped Sonja from the space suit she had not needed, and Glyn fetched her suitcases in from the corridor. He was not exactly gracious. In an emergency, he said, you did not stop to pack enough clothes to stock a boutique, and he refused to go and fetch her vanity case from the apartment. She had to pick the nail polish from her legs. And when, in an attempt to be friendly, she asked Matthew if he had heard the latest Galaxy Hunters album, Glyn told her to shut her mouth because they had more important things to talk about.

It was humiliating.

Sonja hated Glyn.

He was harsh as the light, common Welsh in his maroon uniform. Starship stewards were there to help people, but he was rude to the point of ignorance. She would report him to the personnel officer! He had no right to be in charge of a life ferry. He was not much older than she was and he had no idea how to organize things. There was no crew on board, no catering staff, and no signs of anyone arriving. And Glyn just sat there, his limbs draped across the silver seats, doing nothing! It was like waiting for Christmas.

Sonja complained.

"What the hell do you expect me to do?" Glyn asked her.

"You could go and find someone!"

"If you're so keen, girlie . . ."

"You're the one who's on duty!"

"Why should I take orders from you?"

"Well, we can't stay here on our own, can we?" Sonja said angrily.

"That's true enough," Matthew said.

Glyn rounded on him.

His face looked desperate.

"You got a suggestion to make?"

"I think we have to face it," Matthew said.

"Face what?"

"No one else is coming."

"We can't be the only ones left!" Glyn said.

"Maybe not," said Matthew. "But maybe on this part of the ship we are."

Sonja reached for her space suit.

"In that case," she said decisively, "we'll go to one of the other life ferries."

"No!" Glyn said sharply.

"Why not?"

Glyn prowled the gangway. His fist beat on the palm of his other hand. He knew why not. The *Sky Rider* sealed herself off in sections—A deck, B deck, C deck, D deck, maintenance, education, recreation, crew quarters and control. If the other sections were under vacuum conditions, it would not be possible to reach another life ferry without opening the sealed doors and creating a vacuum here. It was safer to stay as they were. And they were not the only ones left alive on B deck. He remembered seeing a girl earlier on—not Sonja.

"There's a girl," said Glyn. "A blond girl. I saw her turn down the corridor toward the two-bedroom apartments, but I didn't see her come back. She must be still there. And she mightn't be the only one. We've got to check the cabins, see? All of them."

"That could take ages," Matthew said.

"We're not short on time, are we?"

Matthew pondered.

In nature, the strong survived and those who

could not look after themselves deserved to perish. But hidden beneath the folds of his space suit was a plastic container. He would have risked his life to save those butterflies—now he could not refuse to take the responsibility for some unknown girl. He got to his feet.

"What about me?" Sonja asked. "You're not going to leave me here on my own, are you?"

"That's up to you," Glyn said.

Without knowing it Ann was giving up. Blackness floated before her eyes. Gold speckles danced and there was a ringing in her ears. She closed her eyes and the noise went on, ringing sound in her head. Then it was not in her head but outside, the tinkle of sleigh bells or the song of gnats on summer evenings, icicles on trees— sound so distant she could not be sure she heard it. Yet it was there, some faraway music that was nothing to do with her. She opened her eyes.

Beyond the door, in the outer cabin where the shadows were deep and dark, pinpricks of light moved and drifted, floated like dust motes down a shaft of sun, twinkled like scraps of stars. Ann blinked, not believing that she really saw them, but still they were there, small and dancing, clear as piano notes—tiny cadences of light. Light within music, music within light, come together in a kind of song, soft and unearthly. Almost Ann could distinguish the words. She watched and listened.

The light and the music danced and spun, collected like mist and formed into a ball that closed and retreated, as if it wanted her to follow. And a voice in the light that knew no language called her to come. Like one in a trance she left her bed and let the blankets fall to the floor.

The music was full of life, and she too was alive. Her heart beat strong and the blood pulsed through her veins and the shining strands of her disheveled hair were warm and long. She was like the music, alive and knowing. She could leave behind the cold empty room, enter the yellow light and be part of the song. But suddenly it fled, dissolved in the sound of breaking glass, a rush of air and the hiss of the opening door. And the voice Ann heard then was Welsh and human.

"Okay, girlie, let's have your name, rank and number!"

It was an act of vandalism, but it gave them a sense of purpose and they did not need to think about their own problems. They smashed the glass and opened the doors and systematically entered the apartments, as if they had a right to do so, as if they were the only authority left on board the *Sky Rider*. The vast chilly corridors

41

echoed with their voices. In the semidarkness they checked and called and found no one. Then Glyn found the girl.

Sonja pushed past him.

"I know her," Sonja said.

Whoever she was, Glyn thought, she was damned stupid. She had been sealed inside an airtight compartment and not tried to get out. A couple of hours more and she would have been dead. He stared at her. She did not look stupid. Her eyes were clear blue and intelligent enough. But her face was ashen white. She chewed on her lower lip and her gaze passed nervously from one to another waiting for someone to speak.

"What's your name, girlie?" Glyn asked her again.

"Ann Trethowen," Sonja said.

"She can speak for herself, can't she?"

But Matthew sensed her fear.

"We shan't hurt you," he assured her.

"What you doing here, anyway?" Glyn asked.

"Mind your own business," Sonja said.

"I asked her, not you! She should be in school."

"So maybe she was sick."

"What's the matter, girlie?" Glyn asked Ann. "The cat got your tongue, has it?"

Wretched and miserable Ann made no reply.

"Leave her alone," Matthew said.

"Who's touching her?" Glyn asked.

"You'd better take her to the life ferry," Matthew told Sonja.

"Why me?" Sonja asked.

"Because you're the one who knows her, dumbo!" Glyn said.

"I've never even spoken to her before now!"

"I thought you said—"

"I know her name, that's all!"

"Does it matter?" Matthew asked. "All we're asking you to do is help her pack her things and take her to the life ferry."

"And what about *my* things?" Sonja asked. "What about my vanity case and all those cassettes I couldn't carry?"

"I'll fetch the motorized trailer," Glyn said.

Sonja scowled at him and turned to Ann.

"Get your case."

Very slightly Ann lifted her head.

A flush warmed her cheeks.

And her voice came quiet and defiant.

"I'd rather stay here, thank you. I'm waiting for my father."

"Your father won't be coming," Sonja said sourly.

Ann's face blanched. "Why not?"

"I don't believe it!" said Glyn. "She's got no idea."

"Nor have you!" Matthew said harshly.

"There's been a bit of an accident," he said to Ann. "We don't *know* your father's not coming, but he's probably on one of the other decks and the elevators aren't working. So if you'll just collect up your things and go with Sonja . . ."

Ann bit her lip. His voice was kind but he could not persuade her.

"I'd rather wait here," she said.

"I don't think you realize—" Matthew began.

"Leave this to me," Glyn said.

There was nothing kind about Glyn.

His hand gripped Ann's arm.

Gray eyes, hard as flint, gazed into her own.

"Bags!" said Glyn. "Pack 'em! Now! Then get on your bike and beat it! No ifs or buts. If you're not in that life ferry when I get back, then your dad is going to hear about it, see? See!"

Ann saw.

His finger pointed to the door and his voice was ruthless. And she saw their faces in the murky light, unrelenting and out of patience. She had no choice. She had to go with that horrible girl, because if she did not they would make her— even the boy with glasses would make her. Mutely Ann nodded, and Glyn's cruel fingers thrust her away and let go. Meekly she went to pack her suitcase. Her eyes filled with tears, and not long ago she had heard music.

44

5

Ann sat in her coat and hat, perched on the edge of the seat as if she were expecting to leave at any moment. Gloves and a handbag lay beside her and her suitcase stood between her feet. Opposite was the door, the open air lock that led back into the darkening corridors of the *Sky Rider*. Dumped luggage and three empty space suits filled the nearby seats but there was no one else on board. There were no crew, Sonja said, so they would have to go to another life ferry. They would probably go as soon as Glyn and Matthew got back, Sonja said, so there was not much point in Ann's taking her coat off. She sat and waited. Hot lights made her sweat and the thought of

Glyn returning made her afraid, but she had regained her hope. Maybe when they went to the other life ferry her father would be on board it and she would not have to stay with Glyn or Sonja anymore. The thought of leaving them made her happy. She even smiled when Sonja returned from the washroom.

"Do I look all right?" Sonja said anxiously.

She had tidied her short-cropped hair.

And her complexion shone washed and rosy in the light.

Ann nodded.

"I suppose you haven't got any makeup I can borrow?"

"I don't wear makeup," Ann told her.

Sonja shrugged her indifference.

"Mine's in my vanity case," she said. "And I left that behind. I hope they remember to bring it. How long have they been?"

Ann glanced at her watch.

"Half an hour."

"They wouldn't dream of hurrying themselves, of course," Sonja said sourly. "Never mind us. We can just sit here and bite our nails. I bet my mother's halfway back to Earth by now."

Ann looked alarmed. "Won't they wait for us?"

"Of course they'll wait for us," Sonja retorted.

"But you just said . . ."

"I never meant it literally. Good grief! My mother's hardly likely to go without me, is she? And once they've checked the passenger list and found we're missing, they're bound to come looking for us."

"I expect my father's worried," Ann said.

Sonja did not deny it.

It was better to believe it, cling to the conviction. Dependency on parents and adults did not end suddenly in a moment of noise and darkness. Even separated, you went on trusting them. Somewhere Ann's father was worried. And somewhere Sonja's mother was organizing a search party, her booming authoritarian tones bullying people into action. One way or another they were bound to be rescued—with no thanks to Glyn. But it was thanks to Glyn that Ann was here. Sonja glanced at her pale drawn face and sensed an ally.

"Do you like him?" Sonja asked her.

"Who?" said Ann.

"Glyn."

Ann touched the bruised flesh of her upper arm.

Her eyes betrayed nervousness, even fear.

"He's all right," she murmured politely.

"I can't stand him," Sonja said.

Glyn and Matthew paused outside the last cabin.

All along the corridors the doors gaped open.

They had found no one else.

"Is there any point?" Matthew asked.

"You want to spend the rest of your life wondering?" said Glyn.

Matthew shook his head.

For the last time he pulled down the sleeve of his sweater to protect his knuckles and smashed the glass. Broken shards fell to the floor and lay like rubies in the half-light, and the door slid open with a slow sigh. The apartment accommodated six persons, according to Glyn's memory of the passenger list, and they expected it to be empty, like every other apartment. But it was not. In the center of the main floor space a small child stood clutching a furry toy. Her white-fair hair was tied in neat bunches on either side of her head, and she was naked except for her underpants. Quite unperturbed, she stared at them.

"God in heaven," Glyn muttered. "This is all we need."

"Hello," Matthew said brightly. "What's *your* name?"

The small girl scratched her stomach.

"Caroline," she said. "Are you the doctor?"

"No," said Matthew. "Were you expecting him?"

"I've got spots," Caroline announced proudly.

"Have you?"

"All over my tummy and all over my face and all over everywhere. And Benjamin has. Mummy's goned to fetch the doctor. Why hasn't Mummy come back?"

"I expect the doctor was busy," Matthew told her.

The toy dangled by its ear.

There was a brief silence.

"I don't believe this," said Glyn.

"I'm afraid it's true," said Matthew.

"What do we do, for Christ's sake?"

"We'll have to take her with us."

"We can't look after a spotty kid!"

"We can't leave her here," Matthew said reasonably.

Caroline watched them, her head cocked like a bird's, her bright child's eyes missing nothing. She summed them up in seconds. Frowning and hostile, she shuffled closer to the shelter of Matthew's legs. Her voice was belligerent.

"Who's *he*?" she asked, pointing at Glyn.

"That's Glyn," Matthew told her.

"I don't like him," she said fiercely.

"And maybe I don't like you," Glyn growled.

"Which doesn't alter the fact," Matthew said quietly.

He squatted on his heels and gently gripped Caroline's arms. You had to make friends with small children, not antagonize them. And perhaps in a few years Eleanor would look like Caroline, her fat baby limbs turned into a sturdy little girl. The eyes that stared at him were blue and clear, all-seeing and all-knowing. There was no fooling a child like Caroline.

"Do you like *me*?" Matthew asked her.

"Yes," she said.

"Then how would you like to come for a walk with me?"

She looked doubtful.

"There's a ship," said Matthew, "with big silver seats. And I know where to find some chocolate-flavored crackers."

Caroline still looked doubtful.

"Won't you come?" Matthew asked her.

She shook her head.

"Mummy said not to," she told him. "Mummy said to stay here with Benjamin till she fetched the doctor or I'll have my bottom smacked."

"You can bring Benjamin with you," Matthew said. "Shall I carry him for you?"

He took away the blue rabbity toy she was holding. She released it willingly enough but she would not come to his outstretched hand that was waiting to hold hers. And he sensed that he had not understood her correctly, that something important was missing and she was unsure, even now, about telling him. In the long silence while Glyn waited impatiently, Matthew realized he was once more being summed up. Then very slightly Caroline nodded.

"Benjamin's in there," she said.

And pointed to an adjoining room.

Matthew stared at her in alarm, looked down at the toy he was holding.

"Who's this then?"

"That's Uggy," said Caroline.

"Uggy," said Matthew. "And Benjamin's in there?"

Again Caroline nodded.

Matthew got to his feet and looked at Glyn.

"I've got a horrible feeling . . ."

"It's nothing to the feeling I've got, boyo," Glyn said.

Sonja was bored. There was nothing to do on the ferry ship and nothing to talk about. She had tried to talk about music but Ann never listened. All she did was sit there screwing her gloves in her hands and wondering how long it would be before her father came. Sonja got sick of it. Every subject she tried came back to Ann's father. She would not have minded so much if he had been someone special, but he was nothing more than a common agricultural worker. Sonja roamed away, wandered into the control cabin with its mass of meaningless dials and switches. Two plush swivel chairs tempted her to sit in them. She could be both pilot and navigator, but games of pretend did not interest her and the small closed-in room began to bother her. She wandered back down the length of the main cabin. And still Ann sat there, unmoving, unheeding, twisting her gloves in her hand. Sonja was about to say something rude, but three closed doors at the rear end of the ship attracted her attention. One led into the washroom where she had already been, but the other two needed exploring.

"Are you coming?" she asked Ann.

"Where?" said Ann.

"To see what's behind those doors."

Ann looked.

"No thank you," she said. "Someone might come."

"Please yourself," Sonja said cuttingly.

Ann stayed, watching the dark space of the air lock. Just now, between the sounds of Sonja's steps on the floor, she thought she had heard a faint faraway cry. She listened intently but she could hear nothing more from the long corridors, and the hiss of the door being opened eclipsed the silence. No steps, no voices—then, frightening in its loudness, came a clatter of things in the room where Sonja had gone, like metal tools falling against metal walls, rattling banging noises and Sonja's exasperated voice calling her to come.

Reluctantly Ann went. It was a closet containing space suits and oxygen cylinders, strap harnesses, safety ropes and rocket guns. And out of the storage cupboard that Sonja had opened spilled a cascade of tools—axes and hammers, pickaxes and spades, saws and scythes and pitchforks and hoes. Ann helped her replace them.

"What the heck do they want all these for?" Sonja asked.

Ann knew.

They were there for a purpose. Fear gripped her as she maneuvered a plowshare back into place. It was cold steel, and the light shone cruel on its edge. They were instruments of survival. The life ferry carried them just in case—in case of a landfall on some unknown planet. She did not tell Sonja that.

"There's a run in your panty hose," Ann said quietly.

"Oh damn!" Sonja said.

Glyn had not asked for it, but he wore the starship uniform so he had no choice. In the end the responsibility was his. He was responsible for the lives of the others, and Benjamin was the heaviest burden of all. A terrible sinking feeling shot through Glyn's guts. He had no idea how to cater for the needs of a small baby. He stared down at the cot. Disturbed by Caroline's chatter, Benjamin stirred and woke. His small face puckered in the shadowy light and the black gap of his mouth opened like a fish's, issued its final unspeakable demand. Glyn backed away as Benjamin bawled. He was out of his depth here—worse than useless. Abruptly he turned and left the room, but the sound followed him—a shrill angry wail.

Matthew was doing up buttons on Caroline's dress.

"I'll be back in a minute," Glyn said.

He had to get away.

He hãd to think.

It was not just a question of immediate survival and it was more than a suitcase Benjamin would need. He went to fetch the motorized trailer, and the crying that followed him suddenly ceased. His steps trod softly through the silences. Then somewhere, far ahead of him, something crashed, clattered, echoed faintly down the darkening corridor—metallic sounds, repeating and repeating, adding fear to his anxiety. The ship was breaking up. He wanted to run, save his skin in the only way he knew how, but he staved off his panic. He had a child and a baby to consider before himself.

Calmly and unhurriedly he made himself walk until he reached the trailer, and calmly he drove it back to the cabin. The noise of the motor drowned the thud of his heart, but when he switched off the ignition he heard it again, the rattle of metal that was instantly lost in the renewed yelling of the baby. Grimly Glyn began to offload the trailer. A great white mountain of used bed sheets grew in the corridor and Caroline, fully dressed, laughed and climbed it and thought it was a game.

"Beat it!" Glyn said gruffly. "Or else come and help."

Surprisingly, she came. Like a small assistant she worked beside him, hurling the pillowcases into a heap on the floor. She was building her own mountain, she said. But Glyn had no time for games. He knew only the reality—the nearness of death, Benjamin's crying and the stink when he entered the cabin. Matthew was struggling to change the diaper.

"I think we've got two cases of German measles on our hands," Matthew said.

"That's not all we've got," Glyn said grimly.

"Is something wrong?"

"I heard a noise. We got to hurry."

"Pass me that pin," Matthew said.

Glyn opened a cupboard.

They needed things, lots of things. They needed pacifiers and baby bottles and milk powder. Hazy recollections drifted through his mind—Sonja in her garish tunic top and Ann with her pale face and hair the color of moonlight. They seemed to belong to a different reality, a different time, a different space—hours ago in an empty life ferry and part of the past that the baby blotted out. And it made no difference having his diaper changed. He was surrounded by shadows and strange people with strange voices. His mouth stayed open and bawling and he squirmed in Matthew's arms like a fat white grub.

Glyn loaded the trailer with anything that might be applicable to him or Caroline—diapers and bibs, waterproof pants and playsuits, the little girl's undies and nightgowns, unbreakable dishes with pixies, spoons and feeding cups and food. Item by item Caroline cleared the bathroom—talcum powder and cotton, medicine for tummy pains, cream for sore bottoms, teething lotion, nail clippers and a plastic potty for toilet training. There seemed to be no end to Benjamin's needs. But finally Glyn staggered to the trailer with the last load and Matthew looked around.

"I think that's everything."

It was everything except Caroline and Uggy.

It was everything except Benjamin.

56

"Come on, beautiful boy," Matthew said.

Glyn closed his eyes.

With Matthew's words came the final terrible acceptance.

6

"This is Caroline," Matthew announced.

The small girl clung to his hand.

A red angry rash showed on her face.

And she clutched a blue hairy toy with goggle eyes.

"That's Uggy," said Matthew. "And this is Benjamin. We think he's about five months old."

Sonja stared.

Benjamin was sick too, covered with a solid mass of pinprick spots, and the ship was alive with his screaming baby sound. She forgot about Ann. Her voice rose to a horrified shriek.

"What'd you bring them here for?"

Glyn dumped an armful of children's clothes on the nearest seat.

"Where else were we supposed to take them?"

"You should have taken them to the Infirmary!"

"The Infirmary's up the other end of the ship," said Glyn. "And there's no way of getting there. We're sealed off, remember? And they've got as much right to be here as you."

"Well, I'm not looking after them," Sonja said sullenly.

"No one asked you to," Matthew said.

Glyn returned to the trailer for the next load of things, and keeping hold of Caroline's hand, Matthew led her along the gangway to a pair of empty seats. Wet puddled the floor where he had just been standing, and Benjamin squealed and struggled in his arms like a stuck pig.

"Oh look, Mattoo," said Caroline. "Benjamin's weed."

Matthew knew.

He had felt the wet warmth seep through his trousers.

"I'll have to change him," Matthew said.

Sonja wrinkled her nose in disgust.

"You're not going to change him in here, are you?"

Matthew ignored her.

59

"Find me a clean diaper and some cotton," he said to Caroline.

Obediently, Caroline went. Keeping a wary eye on Sonja she sidled past her, ran through the air lock to join Glyn. Between Benjamin's screams they heard her breathless voice relaying the message and Glyn's gruff reply.

"We can't find none, Mattoo!" Caroline shouted back.

"On the bottom shelf!" Matthew told her.

"What?" said Glyn.

Benjamin howled.

"Doesn't he ever shut up?" Sonja asked.

Matthew sighed and looked at Ann.

She sat dumb and watching on the edge of the seat.

"I suppose you wouldn't like to hold Benjamin whilst I go and . . ." Ann bent her head. "No," said Matthew, "I should have known you wouldn't."

"And you needn't ask me!" Sonja said.

"Give him to me, boyo," said Glyn.

He dumped the load of clothes and took the baby. Five minutes ago he would not have touched Benjamin if Matthew had paid him, but now he did it out of sheer defiance. Benjamin screamed and struggled. A trickle of regurgitated milk flowed white down the front of Glyn's uniform. Wetness soaked through his arm. He was stinking of sourness and urine but still he held

60

on. And they should be doing this, Ann and Sonja, not him! But they were useless, both of them. Stupid useless girls! His resentment simmered. First Class labels glared red on Sonja's suitcases, and Matthew took back the baby. Matthew was the only one who showed any degree of human concern.

"Manage, can you, boyo?" Glyn asked anxiously.

He could manage.

Assisted by Caroline, who handed him the things he needed, he seemed to know exactly what he was doing. This was no stumbling effort in the half-light, but a fast precision process. Glyn watched. He made it look easy. Pink liquid and cotton cleaned up Benjamin's exposed parts. He was dusted with talcum powder, his spotty bottom treated with ointment and quickly covered up. There was nothing to it. But Matthew did not stop there. He strapped Benjamin to a seat and into his fat grasping fist he put a chocolate-flavored cracker. Half sitting, half lying, Benjamin looked at it with interest, then jammed it into his mouth. Like a little red-faced cherub, he smiled and sucked. Soft, contented sounds gurgled in his throat and all the cabin turned beautifully quiet and still.

"You make me feel ignorant, boyo," Glyn said softly.

Matthew sat back on his heels.

"It's not difficult when you know how."

"Got a way with babies, haven't you?"

"My sister has one."

"I couldn't have done it, not like that."

"I guess we all have our uses," Matthew said.

"Yes," said Glyn. "It's finding them that's the trouble." He looked at Sonja. There was a supercilious expression on her face and her lips showed scorn. She patted a stray end of hair into place with her pink painted nails. "And you're not sitting there like a flipping ornament!" Glyn told her. "I want something to eat!"

Next to the closet where the space suits were kept was a kind of kitchen-cum-storeroom. It was long and narrow, like a hallway, and on either side, from floor to ceiling, cupboards lined the walls. The only open space was occupied by a sink unit and work counter. Strange-looking transparent urns with chrome fittings were fixed to the wall over it, and a small first-aid cupboard was marked with a red cross. Sonja leaned against the closed door. She was pale and shaking and her voice was venomous.

"I hate him!" Sonja said.

Ann bit her lip. Her cheeks burned and Glyn's words cut her like shame. He had called her a stuffed dummy and ordered her to go with Sonja, and now she was here she did not know what to do or say. She stood with the misery inside her, in the vent of Sonja's fury, feeling her own uselessness, her own inadequacy.

"I'd like to kill him!" Sonja said. "Who the hell does he think he is?"

He was a boy in a maroon uniform—a starship steward. He had the authority. On board the life ferry he gave the orders and Sonja was expected to obey.

"He'll be sorry when this is over," Sonja said. "I'll tell my mother about him. She'll see he gets fired for the way he's spoken to me. You wait!" She flung open the nearest cupboard. "Soup!" she said, and moved onto the next. "More soup!" She slammed it shut. "Don't just stand there!" she said to Ann. "We have to find something to eat, don't we?"

Ann felt sick, sick and afraid. Sick with nerves and sick for her father. It was hours now since the accident. They ought to be in the communal dining room, not here. Here there was only soup, boxes and boxes of it—chicken and oxtail, tomato and mushroom, minestrone and vegetable, lentil and pea. The cupboards were full of it, and instructions on how to make it were printed on notices on the insides of the doors, along with menus for a balanced diet. It was not luxury the life ferry catered for, just need—roughage and protein and vitamins, rye bread and bran biscuits, fruit and milk and powdered orange. Ann opened another cupboard. Hundreds and hundreds of packets of dried fruit were stacked on the shelves—figs and prunes and apple rounds, raisins and apricots and dried fruit salad.

"It says soak one hour in cold water," Ann said.

Sonja dumped a pack of rye bread on the counter.

"There's not even any butter!"

"I expect you're supposed to dip it in the soup," Ann said.

Sonja sniffed. "How uncivilized!"

"Well, there doesn't seem to be anything else to eat."

"Have you ever made soup?" Sonja asked.

"No," said Ann.

"In that case," said Sonja, "he can jolly well get his own!"

The door to the kitchen closed behind Ann and Sonja.

Matthew tied a bib under Benjamin's chin.

"I assume you want to talk," he said to Glyn.

"I want a cracker, Mattoo," said Caroline.

"If you wait a minute," Matthew told her, "the girls will be getting you something to eat."

"I don't want somefink in a minute! I want it now!"

Caroline's voice was fierce and demanding.

"Here!" said Glyn. He took a cracker from the packet and handed it to her. "Take it and shut up!"

Matthew sank wearily into the seat next to Benjamin. Light on the white walls played hard on his eyes and the cabin clock showed 2025 hours. He checked his watch. It was only 17:10 but he could no longer work out the difference. Time had gone mad, turned into a chaos without order, a perpetual present which was slowly ticking away. There had been an accident on board the *Sky Rider* but somehow it seemed not to matter. The urgency was gone. Only Glyn seemed worried—pacing up and down along the gangway.

"We got to do something," Glyn said.

"Like what?" Matthew asked.

"She could break up, you know."

"You were pretty hard on her."

"Who?"

"Ann."

"Damn Ann," said Glyn. "I'm talking about the *Sky Rider*."

Ann and Sonja, Caroline and the baby—it was not people who worried Glyn, it was circumstance. He had heard the sound of metal falling, inside the ship, not half an hour ago. Matthew frowned. Something was wrong with that. You could not base a conclusion on partial knowledge. His mind sharpened, struggled with the concept of disintegration and the material laws that governed space. Outside was a vacuum and zero gravity. Unless impelled by internal or external forces things stayed motionless, in free fall. As it was in the moment after the impact, so it was now and always would be. There was no chance of the *Sky Rider* breaking up.

"You sure, are you?" Glyn asked him.

"No," said Matthew.

There was only one certainty. They were six people alone in a life ferry. Beyond their own immediate existence they could not be sure of anything and neither could they guess. For all they knew, the *Sky Rider* could still be intact, burning with lights and life, blazing her trail to the stars.

"There's only one way to find out," Matthew said.

Glyn knew.

One of them would have to go.

"I want to sit on your lap, Mattoo," Caroline said.

And it would not be Matthew who went.

There was a churning hollow in Glyn's guts. He did not know if it was fear or hunger, but he knew how to eliminate the one possibility. He entered the kitchen. Ann and Sonja leaned against the sink unit. They had done nothing, either of them. Doors to the store cupboards gaped open. Sealed packets littered the counter. There was soup and prunes and something that looked like dog biscuits, but they had done nothing about it.

"Out of the way!" Glyn said angrily.

Sonja moved and Ann retreated, her blond hair melting into the light at the far end of the room. Grim and unspeaking, Glyn read the instructions on the packet and silently they watched him. He measured five scoopsful of powder into one of the urns and pressed the button. Water hissed into it, boiling hot, clouding the glass. It rose, tomato red, creeping up the lines of liquid capacity. Full, it might have fed fifty people, but Glyn only made a couple of pints, switched on the agitator, waited one minute and switched off. They watched him reach for a plastic cup. Thick soup spewed from the dispenser in a measured amount. With a cup of soup in one hand and a rye biscuit in the other, Glyn returned to the main cabin.

Sonja hated him. But her stomach was hungry for the rich soupy smell.

"Did you see how he worked it?" she asked Ann.

Ann shook her head.

Sonja picked up a cup for herself. Bright chrome fittings gave her no clue. She fiddled and failed and tried again. Finally she succeeded. She pushed up a lever and the soup flowed, a steaming jet that sprayed on the counter and trickled onto the floor.

"Find something to clean it up," she told Ann.

Ann remembered seeing a metal bucket in the closet where the space suits were kept. She went to find it, but when she opened the cupboard everything fell out again, hoes and axes and pick-axes, with a hideous clatter of sound. For the second time she bent to put them away, and behind her was a shadow, dark in the light and closing in on her. Fearfully she turned to look. Her heart thudded in her rib cage and she cowered away from Glyn's voice.

"It was you, wasn't it? You! You great clumsy cow! You done that before, didn't you?"

7

The moment Glyn had been dreading finally arrived and he could no longer postpone it. He buttoned his jacket.

"I'll just go and see what's what then," Glyn said.

Sonja picked up her suitcases.

"We may as well all come."

"It's best if Glyn goes alone," Matthew said.

"Why?"

"Check things out first, see?" Glyn said. "I'll come back for you."

"Good luck," Matthew said simply.

Glyn nodded. "I shan't be long."

He did not want to go. Fear clawed his nerves. He was afraid of what he would find, but he had no choice. An imperative drove him, and on all their faces was a look of expectancy. They depended on him for their lives. Sheer courage made him turn away from the warmth and safety of the small ship. He stepped through the air lock and was alone. He did not look back.

Dark and empty, the *Sky Rider* stretched out before him and the light made a bridge going into it. He could see nothing beyond. He went like a blind man following the walls, feeling his way with slow shuffling steps. But gradually his eyes grew accustomed and the lights had not totally faded. The spent batteries still gave a faint trace of illumination. The *Sky Rider* split into dim perspectives, a shine of ceilings and floors. He could see the corridor looming ahead of him, converging like a tunnel into blackness, and the red glint of the arrows that pointed the way back.

Glyn walked on, past the conjunctions of corridors that led to the cabins, toward the elevators and the stairs and the main thoroughfare that gave access to the other decks and apartments. The silence unnerved him. His steps were too loud. They betrayed his presence and he felt that he had no right to be there. He had the absurd feeling he was not alone. He stopped to listen. The emptiness was intense, almost a tangible quality, and the sensing grew stronger.

Something or someone out in the darkness knew he was there. But he heard and saw nothing and walked on. Then again he stopped. It was closer now, watching him, waiting for him, silent and unseen. But again there was nothing.

"Imagination, boyo," Glyn told himself.

He turned the last corner.

And what he saw then had nothing to do with imagination. Way up ahead of him was a ball of light. His heart missed a beat, restarted wildly; and a sickening fear clutched his stomach. But the light did not move. It stayed where it was, hovering by the elevators, waiting for him to approach. And very faintly he thought he could hear music—tiny bell-like sounds, like morris dancers at the Welsh eisteddfod, incongruous and out of place. Music and light—Glyn stared at it. For a moment he thought of turning back.

"Can't hurt you though, can it?" Glyn reasoned.

The light shimmered.

Within the sphere of brightness tiny particles whirled and spun. It looked harmless enough—some strange phenomenon he had not come across before, like ball lightning. Step by slow step Glyn advanced, watching it, daring it to move. But it stayed suspended, just where it was, and gradually he lost his fear. He had other, more important things to think about.

Double doors barred his entry to the main

sections of the ship and sealed off the stairs. Through the round porthole windows he could see darkness, but then he had hardly expected to find a blaze of light and a quick return to normality. Here, like everywhere else, the red words glowed with the same instructions. Glyn did not need to read them. He pulled down the sleeve of his jacket, clenched his fist to smash the glass and release the suction. It was automatic. His arm raised and his eye took aim. But something moved at the corner of his vision, came at him, straight and fast, a shriek of sound and light.

The shock struck him, high-voltage electric, hurling him backward across the corridor. He fell hard against the opposite wall, lay dazed for a moment wondering how he had got there. Pain prickled his arm. He thought he had been struck by a fist in the small of his back and he wanted to cry like a baby. And the light had changed its shape. It stood now like a pillar of pale-yellow flame, its soft fragile music playing on. Beautiful and menacing, it had positioned itself between Glyn and the door, and he sensed it would not let him through.

"Why?" Glyn asked it.

Nothing answered him.

There was no voice amid the light. But suddenly a thought touched Glyn's mind. He felt the horror inside him. If he had smashed the glass and released the suction he could have been dead—and they too could have been dead, Ann and Sonja, Matthew, Caroline and the baby—killed by his action.

That pale fire had saved him from committing mindless murder.

"Did you know that?" Glyn asked it.

The flame trembled.

Its music was soft and sad, like leaves in an autumn breeze, telling him nothing. It drew aside, shrank once more to a ball of light and slowly faded. A few prickles of gold danced by the elevator doors and seeped away into the darkness. The bell sounds ceased and Glyn was alone again. There was nothing to protect him now. Warily he pressed his face against the porthole.

He saw darkness and stars.

He saw the *Sky Rider*.

She had been torn apart. Rooms and corridors ended a few feet away. Jagged walls opened onto empty space. Walkways and floors led into nowhere. Twisted girders hung suspended over a yawning abyss and great chunks of her hull slowly revolved, hurtling outward and onward into the universe. Her wreckage stretched for miles. And among it floated the bodies of people, dead and drifting in a graveyard of stars. Glyn stared. Something white brushed the window, a human hand that tapped and tapped, asking to be let in. A face gazed up at him, a dead man's face with open mouth and staring eyes, frozen forever in an expression of terror. They were dead, all of them, twelve hundred people all come together and contained in the hideous unmoving stare of a single man.

With a choked cry Glyn turned away. He went running, stumbling, back along the corridor. And the man went with him, a face in his memory, the brutal impact of death. He wanted to scream and thrust it from him. He wanted to scream in the loneliness. They were dead! They were dead! And no one could help him. And the face was trapped in his mind.

They heard footsteps running and Glyn reeled through the door like someone drunk, clutched at the seat to stop himself falling. They had one quick glimpse of his white stricken face before he entered the washroom and closed the door behind him. Sonja and Matthew looked at each other in alarm. They heard retching sounds and a stifled sobbing. Something was wrong! Matthew's expression turned grim. His lips tightened and he did not hesitate. He dumped Benjamin in Ann's lap. She was pale and frightened and she did not want to hold him, but Matthew had no choice, and neither did she.

"Look after him," Matthew told her.

He was going to Glyn.

"I want to come with you, Mattoo," Caroline said.

"No," said Matthew. "You stay here."

Her voice rose to a wail. "I want to come!"

Matthew looked at Sonja.

"Don't let her follow me," he said.

Caroline screamed as Sonja grabbed her arm, but already Matthew was gone into the washroom with the door closed behind him. He heard the pound of her small fists as he leaned against it, but it dissolved in the sound of water that swilled down the basin and Glyn's dry sobbing. With his head on his arm he rested against the wall, locked in his grief and despair. Matthew watched helplessly. There was nothing he could say. He watched as the free fist beat, a thud of flesh against metal that was repeated and repeated, each time more violently, as if by the pain of it Glyn was killing some other, greater pain. And gradually the sobbing ceased and the action took over, regular and monotonous the clenched fist smashed against the wall. Viciously, relentlessly, Glyn continued. His breathing grew deep and harsh. His split knuckles bled. It was as if he pitched the whole of his being into it. Matthew stepped forward, gripped Glyn's wrist and wrestled for stillness.

"That's enough!" Matthew said firmly.

He expected a reaction.

He expected the violence to turn on him. But slowly the clenched muscles relaxed and the tension eased. The arm fell limply and there was no more fight. Matthew released his hold and turned off the tap. Only their breathing disturbed the silence, and the muffled crying of children in the outer cabin. In the aftershock of extreme emotion Glyn sank slowly to the floor, sat with his head against the wall, staring at nothing. His face was ghastly white and he was shivering violently.

"They're dead, boyo," Glyn said hopelessly. "All of 'em."

"What about the other life ferries?" Matthew asked.

"I don't know."

"There could be others who've . . . ?"

"If there are," said Glyn, "there's no way of reaching them."

"Not even if we wore space suits?"

"She's blown apart," Glyn said dully.

"We're on our own then?"

Glyn nodded.

A glimmer of tears showed in his eyes.

Matthew looked at his drawn face and broken expression and something twisted inside him, sharp as a sword, an unbearable pity. Whatever Glyn must have seen was something terrible, beyond imagination. He wanted to ask. He wanted to take away the grief and the anguish. But his features hardened. There was no time for sympathy, no time to dwell on the meaning or the loss. The dead were dead, but they had to consider the needs of the living.

When Matthew returned to the cabin, Glyn remained in the washroom. Matthew did not say what was wrong with Glyn. He did not say anything. He just took Benjamin from Ann and hushed his crying, and Caroline dragged her hand free of Sonja's and went to him. He did not say anything to her either. With Benjamin on his lap and one arm around Caroline, he sat on the edge of the seat and slowly rocked her, backward and forward. The motion soothed her and soothed him too. It was as if they comforted each other. His chin rested lightly on her head and his fingers played with her hair. She cuddled against him and was happy. For her the past was forgotten and the future did not concern her, and death meant nothing. But Sonja was not so easily satisfied.

"What's happening now?" Sonja asked.

"Nothing," said Matthew.

"What do you mean—nothing? What about the other life ferries? Did Glyn find anyone? We're not going to stay here all night, are we?"

Matthew looked down at the baby in his lap, stroked the thin fine hair. It was matted with chocolate. In a minute he would have to make him clean. There was a smell about him and his diaper was damp again. Whatever the circumstances, bodily functions went on, physical needs had to be catered to. Twelve hundred people had died and Glyn cracked up, but Benjamin continued undisturbed, a routine of thirst and hunger, refueling and emptying out. And the clock said it was 21:43 but his watch said . . .

"I asked you a question!" Sonja said.

"Yes," said Matthew.

"Yes what?"

"Yes, we will probably be staying here all night."

They would have to sleep on the couches, bunk down with no privacy. Caroline yawned and Benjamin stayed fretful. He needed a bath and his evening feed, and his eyes watered in the harsh light. Matthew tried to get his mind together, tried to recall his sister and Eleanor . . .

"Why can't we go now?" Sonja demanded.

"Because we have to talk about it first," Matthew told her.

"We can talk about it now, can't we?"

"Not without Glyn."

Sonja stared at the washroom door.

"What's wrong with him anyway?"

"He's been sick."

"Not that sick as he can't talk, surely?"

"Just leave him alone!" Matthew said.

"I've a good mind to go on my own!" Sonja said angrily.

Matthew leaned back.

His eyes behind his glasses were quiet and thoughtful.

"So why don't you?" he said.

"All right!" Sonja said. "I will! I'll go on my own and blow Glyn!" She looked at Ann. "Are you coming?"

Ann bent her head.

Her hair was fair as Caroline's, but unlike Caroline she was old enough to understand and Matthew did not need to tell her. People were dead and Glyn had found them and they were trapped here, maybe forever. And her father would never come to take her away because he was dead too. Eyes did not lie. When she looked at Matthew his eyes told her the truth. A deep terrible sympathy passed from him into her. He was dumb and desperate and he needed help as much as she did. Ashen-faced, Ann stared at him. She knew what she had to do. She took off her coat and hat and draped them across the seat. Her voice was steady when she spoke to Sonja and her expression gave nothing away.

"I'm staying here," Ann said firmly.

8

Sonja's arguments were bitter and angry, but neither Ann nor Matthew would leave the life ferry and she would not go alone into the cold empty corridors of the *Sky Rider*. She was scared of the dark and scared of the loneliness and no one would listen. She followed Ann into the kitchen, where she went to mix Benjamin some milk. But whatever she said made no difference. On Ann's drawn pale face there was no response. But her hands trembled. Milk powder spilled on the counter and she was afraid to work the mixing machine.

"Give it to me!" Sonja said furiously.

She whisked the milk and filled the baby bottle, returned to the cabin and gave it to Matthew. But Benjamin refused to feed. The measles rash was on his face now, red and puffy, and his eyes watered. He scrubbed at them with his fists and turned his head away and his irritable crying went on and on. He was not only sick, he was sickening. They must be mad to go on staying here, Sonja thought. And Caroline too was irritable. Uggy's diaper had fallen off and his stiff stuffed arms refused to fit into one of Benjamin's cardigans. She stamped her feet and threw him onto the floor. He lay below the seat with an inane grin fixed on his hairy face. Sonja picked him up, but once more Caroline threw him away.

"Don't want him!" Caroline said rudely.

She turned to Matthew.

She was frowning and aggressive, like a small thug.

"I want to sit on your lap, Mattoo."

Matthew sighed.

He was trying to feed the baby.

Inside Sonja something snapped.

"You're going to bed!" she said to Caroline.

"I'm not! I'm not!" Caroline shrieked.

"We'll see about that," Sonja said grimly. "Find her nightgown," she said to Ann. "And bring the soap and flannel and a towel. Come on, you!"

She grabbed Caroline by the arm and hauled her through to the washroom. Glyn was there, sitting on the floor with his head on his knees. He looked up when Sonja entered. A brief wild anger showed in his eyes but he did not speak. He just left the room—left her to deal with a screaming struggling child and never offered to help.

"Ignorant pig!" Sonja shouted. "And if you don't stop it," she said to Caroline, "I shall give you a damned good hiding! My hand around your backside! You'll have reason to scream!"

But Caroline's screams grew louder, and it was not Ann who came. Matthew had strapped the baby to a seat and left him to cry. Now, infinitely firm, infinitely gentle, he dealt with Caroline. There were no threats, no recriminations. His patience seemed endless. Oblivious to her noise, he stripped her and washed her and toweled her dry. And finally she stood sobbing in her nightgown, wanting her mother. Her mother was gone, but Matthew took her in his arms. She was only a child. She needed love, not spanking.

A lump came to Sonja's throat and she turned away. Her mother was gone too, but there was no one to love *her*. In the comfortless cabin Glyn sat with his back to her, brooding at the wall, Benjamin screamed and Ann stared at the floor, hunched and miserable. It was as if all their loneliness were come together in Sonja. Contagious despair . . . she could feel it in the dumb silences between Benjamin's cries, see it in Glyn's unmoving stance and Ann's bowed head. She could feel it in herself too, a kind of hopelessness, a kind of giving up.

"We can't stay here," Sonja said. "We can't—not on our own."

Only Matthew seemed unaffected.

He went on as if he had lived all his life aboard the ferry and had known no other place. Cheerful and efficient, he washed away Benjamin's stale baby smell, soothed him with words and affection and a bowl of warm water, talked to Caroline and put the soiled diapers to soak in the bucket Ann had found. Sonja sat and waited. Caroline's incessant chatter was childish and futile. Her footsteps pattered in the light. Those small activities were mocking and irrelevant, and all that was important stayed unspoken and festered inside her.

"For Christ's sake!" Sonja shouted. "At least let's talk about it!"

"Oh, look," said Matthew to Caroline.

"You're going all blue, Mattoo," Caroline said.

The lights on the life ferry were time controlled, turning dim blue, like night in the corridors of the *Sky Rider*. The change was beautiful.

Matthew felt as though his eyes were being bathed in balm, his mind, too, washed by the blue light with all his responsibilities fading away. Faces grew soft as the skies of Earth with indigo eyes, and Ann's hair shone like moonlight on still water. White and harsh was the light in the other rooms and in the control cabin, but here it was blue, dissolving all things to shadows, and the seats glowed silver and softly reclined.

"I guess that's it," Matthew said.

"What do you mean?" Sonja asked.

"We go to sleep now."

"That clock's hours wrong!"

"Does it matter?"

"We've got to do something, haven't we? We can't just go to bed and pretend nothing's happened. We've got to decide!"

But Matthew had already decided.

The light was too dim to see by and sleep offered a way out—the cessation of thought, the alleviation of tension, the chance to forget. Spread-eagled across two seats Glyn looked asleep already, and Benjamin had stopped his crying. Matthew rolled him in a shawl and secured him with a safety strap. Sonja could do as she pleased. In the couch next to Caroline Matthew settled himself in the sapphire darkness and waited for the final silence. He heard Glyn snoring. He heard Sonja muttering as she padded about. He heard Ann's stifled sobbing. And maybe it was not so easy to forget.

Ann awoke in the small blue hours of night, intent and listening. The ship was still and intensely cold. Her breath smoked in the silence and on the walls was a sheen of blue ice. Her whole body was numb and frozen, and her lungs breathed in the thin air and failed to be satisfied. Gold speckles danced before her eyes, retreated and were gone. And faintly, just as before, Ann heard music, sharp and clear—the icy tinkling of bells. She sat up.

Over by the air-lock door was a nebulous ball of light.

She glanced around the cabin. Everyone slept. They slept as the oxygen drained away into the black empty hulk of the *Sky Rider*. Such deadly cold—they would die of it soon. Die as the blue air thinned, frosted their faces and froze the breath in their lungs.

The music knew that. It called her to go, enter the light and close the air-lock door. The coat that covered her slipped to the floor. She left her seat and walked in a dream through the blue spaces. And the light turned to a flame of warmth that came to meet her and the music sang in her mind. She stood on the threshold to the *Sky Rider*. It was black as a grave but she was alive and could not mourn. She could only obey the sounds in her head, the pale touch of fire that guided her hand to ensure their survival.

The outer door thudded shut. She sealed the inner door and emptied the air lock, listened to the air pumps working—monotonous, mechanical, a throbbing of sound. There were voices behind her, shrill and meaningless, but she did not heed them. She watched the pressure gauge, the pointer dropping toward the red area and coming to rest. Zero pressure. They were safe now. She released the switch and the pumps stopped. A vacuum stood between them and the *Sky Rider,* and the light and the music fled. Ann turned to face them—blue horrified faces that watched her in the gloom.

"What the hell do you think you're doing?" Glyn asked angrily.

"She's shut the doors!" Sonja raved. "We can't get out now!"

"Cold, Mattoo," Caroline whimpered. "I'm all cold."

"It's okay," Matthew said quickly.

"Is it heck!" Glyn shouted.

"Just take it easy," Matthew told him.

"Easy?" said Glyn. "Easy! You know what she's done, boyo? We're cut off from everything, thanks to her! What right did she have? Who gave her permission? For Christ's sake!" He turned to Ann. His voice was savage and breathless. "Why'd you do it? Why?"

She backed away.

There was no reason anymore.

"Leave her!" Matthew said sharply.

"I'll flaming kill her!" Glyn said.

He gripped her wrist.

A cruel twist of her arm made her cry out.

"You're hurting me! You're hurting me!"

"You stupid meddling cow! I'll break your blasted . . ."

"Let go of her!" Matthew shouted.

"Keep out of it!"

"I'll not stand by . . ."

"She's asked for it!" Sonja screamed.

"Cold," sobbed Caroline. "All cold."

"You going to tell me?" Glyn said to Ann. "You going to tell me why—"

"Music!" Ann wept. "I heard music!"

"Let her go! Let her go!" Matthew insisted.

"Music!"

"What?"

"Let her go!"

Glyn released her.

She stood in the frozen silence.

Tears rolled down her face.

"What's that you said?" Glyn asked her.

But she turned and ran, blundered away down the gangway and into the control cabin.

In a silver chair, with the pain throbbing in her arm, Ann sat and cried for all that had happened, and she did not care who heard her.

Music, she had said. She had heard music. Glyn stared after her. A memory stirred in his mind. And suddenly he knew what Ann had done and why she had done it. On the walls there was melting ice, turning to moisture and slowly condensing. The room was full of blue mist. The life ferry had been supplementing the whole section of the *Sky Rider*, its heat and air seeping away. There was a pain in his chest and his face and hands were frozen.

"Cold, cold," Caroline kept saying.

Glyn looked at the others.

Ann had saved their lives.

"She done right," Glyn said quietly.

"Which is more than you did," Matthew said.

"I don't understand," said Sonja.

9

It was the shivering middle of the night, but they were awake, so the day began again in the lighted control cabin where they gathered and talked, drank cupfuls of hot soup and waited for the atmosphere to warm. But into her own mind Ann withdrew, pale faced and silent, and there was nothing Glyn could say or do to make amends. If it really was music she had heard she would not tell of it, not even to Matthew. And Sonja grew more and more impatient. It was twelve hours now since the accident had happened and all they did was sit and wait for someone to come and find them. And later, when the blue dark ended in the main cabin and Benjamin awoke, they were all feeling tired from lack of sleep.

The hours went on and on, alternating between outbursts of conversation and awkward silences. Ann sat by herself and would not speak. Glyn and Sonja quarreled incessantly and Matthew seemed quiet and enervated, a failed authority who could not be bothered to keep order. There was nothing to do—only care for Caroline and the baby and their own bodily needs, an unvarying routine of soup and soaked fruit and bran biscuits, dirty diapers, feeding times and trouble with Uggy. Caroline's spots improved, a fading redness that left no mark, but her childish prattle was a source of irritation and her boundless energy drove them mad. Nerves frayed and tempers snapped and the tension of waiting dragged on through the unrelieved time. They could stay in the life ferry for years, Glyn said, and already it seemed like years they had been there. White walls surrounded them, unrelenting light on smooth surfaces. Spaces shrank and closed in on them. There was nowhere to go, nowhere to get away from each other. Bad habits got magnified out of all proportion. Ann sniveled. Matthew kept breathing on his glasses and polishing them. Sonja picked at the varnish on her nails and Glyn belched.

"Do you have to make those disgusting noises?" Sonja asked.

"Yes," said Glyn.

"You've got no manners!"

"For pity's sake!" said Matthew. "Don't start again."

"He's supposed to be a starship steward!"

"What's that got to do with it?" Glyn said.

"So how much longer are we going to sit here and do nothing?"

"There's nothing we *can* do."

"We could radio for help!"

"Could we?" Matthew asked Glyn.

"What's the point?" said Glyn.

He reasoned it out. Back on Earth, back at the space station, they were bound to know something had happened. Within the solar system the *Sky Rider* would have kept in touch, regular transmissions from a scheduled flight—like international air transport or the railway systems. You could not lose a transatlantic jet or the two-ten train from London to Cardiff. Once they lost contact with the *Sky Rider*, the space rescue services would be alerted. It was only a matter of waiting, a matter of time before help arrived.

"I suppose you are right," Matthew said wearily.

"We might be here for weeks!" Sonja protested.

"In that case we may as well get used to it," Glyn said.

"It's so damned boring!"

"Boredom is a state of mind," Matthew told her.

"It wouldn't be so bad if we had some pop music," Sonja said.

"I can sing pop music," Caroline offered. "Mummy singed it to Benjamin. 'Hey baby, give your kisses to me. . . .'" Her voice was shrill and tuneless. She swayed on the spot and swung Uggy by his ear. "'I'm wanting your loving and I want it for free. . . .'"

"Turn it off!" Glyn growled.

"She's only singing," Matthew said.

"It's a racket!"

"It's not hurting you, is it?"

"There's bound to *be* a radio," Sonja said.

"Sure," said Glyn. "And who amongst us is going to mess with that control cabin? You?"

Sonja looked at Ann.

She sat alone at the other end of the gangway and picked at the stitching in the hem of her skirt. She had been there for hours, isolated and apart. Matthew had tried talking to her but she had answered only with a shrug of her shoulders or a nod or shake of her head, wordless gestures that had caused him to give up. Best leave her alone, Matthew had said. But now Sonja looked

92

toward her, as if Ann knew things no one else knew, as if she had access to some kind of unknown power.

"Ann might know where the radio is," Sonja said hopefully.

"Stuff that!" said Glyn.

"She closed the air lock, didn't she?"

"What was that music she heard, anyhow?" Matthew asked.

Glyn guessed.

Ball lightning in an empty corridor.

And the sound of bells.

"Some kind of freak phenomenon," Glyn said.

"We could at least ask her," Sonja said.

But Ann's loneliness lay like a gulf between them and Glyn could not cross it. Hunched and silent, she stayed apart and the sight of her was like a punishment. He could not stand it. He left the room to make himself some more soup—and sometimes he had the uneasy feeling he was being watched.

It was still there somewhere, inside the ship, light lost in light. Now and then Ann thought she saw it, but when she looked it was gone, dissolved into solid visual things—the shine of seats and floors and walls, and the shimmer of heat from the air vents. And now and then she thought she heard among the hum of wires and electrical circuits, the hiss of the air conditioning and the murmur of voices, the faraway chiming of bells, tiny sounds that disturbed her thoughts and made her forget about her father, the ache in her arm and the fear she felt. Her heart thumped in hope or alarm but always the illusion fled. And then she caught them watching her, Glyn and Sonja, as if they were expecting something.

She bent her head.

She did not want to remember them.

The length of the cabin made her separate and the hours dragged on, long and lonely. It seemed like years ago she had lived with her father aboard the *Sky Rider,* but she heard Matthew say it was only twenty-four hours. Time was meaningless anyway, just endless waiting without future or past. They would go on forever like this—an unchanging present of Sonja's complaints, Glyn's aggression, Caroline's chatter and Benjamin's bouts of crying. Reality grew more and more like a dream. Tiredness and misery sucked at Ann's mind. Her eyelids grew heavy and all their voices were unintelligible. She dozed and woke. Someone had wrapped her coat around her shoulders and on the floor by her feet was a cup of cold soup. A long way away down the perspectives of light Caroline was screaming and Sonja was shouting, but the sounds they made were remote as birdcalls through the warm summery air and once more Ann slept.

When she awoke it was night. The light was dim blue in the cabin behind her and everyone slept, but next to her, in the control cabin, she heard music. A strange thrill quickened her senses. It was not an illusion this time. It was really there. Clear and unmistakable, beyond the shadow line that crossed her legs, through the door where the brightness flashed in the air like sheet lightning, she heard music—the same sweet tinkling of bells. She wanted to wake the others. She wanted to say, Listen, oh listen. But she was afraid it would slip away, fade in the sound of their voices and be gone.

She entered the control cabin alone. And the light came to meet her—a cloud of particles golden and dancing, growing tall into a pillar of yellow flame. And the music played on the strings of her nerves, not words but emotions— love and courage, fearlessness and strength, sorrow and gentleness all mixed up together. It sang in her mind of beauty and pain. It sang of a terror she did not understand and led her toward it.

The swivel chairs waited, invited her to sit. Without pilot or navigator the life ferry was uncontrolled. Attached to the *Sky Rider* it hurtled on and they were trapped inside it, not knowing

95

what was out there, blind to the stars. In the heart of the light and the music Ann took her seat and reached for the switches. Warm and gold the light touched her hands, a glowing flickering aura of fire that closed and surrounded her. What she did then was an act of faith.

Glyn heard the noise. It was a thunderous metallic sound, grinding through his sleep, reverberating through the walls and floors until the whole ship echoed it. He leaped to his feet. Caroline was screaming—the big bangs had woken her—but her terror was drowned in the next barrage of sound. In the blue light Sonja moved in a shock of fear, stubbed her toe on the seat fixture and clutched at the pain.

"Get out of the way!" Glyn told her.

Matthew groped for his glasses.

"What's going on?" he asked Glyn. "What's she doing?"

Glyn did not know what Ann was doing.

But whatever it was she had no right.

A terrible anger rose inside him.

He ran the length of the gangway but he could not stop her. In the last shock of sound he entered the control cabin and his anger died. Very briefly Glyn was in time to see. She sat in one of the silver chairs, a girl haloed with light. Brighter than the brightness the pale flames surrounded her, pulsed like a heartbeat, tongues of fire touching her hands and her hair. Almost he thought he could make out the vague shape of some other being mingling with hers, limbs and torso, misty and immaterial—a vision of someone so beautiful it hurt. But it fled the moment he saw it. Fragments of music, bitter and sweet, faded with the last echoes of noise and were gone into silence.

Sonja came hobbling into the cabin.

Her voice was loud and harsh.

"What's she done?"

"What's it look like?" Glyn said quietly.

"Oh my God!" said Sonja.

"May He have mercy," Matthew murmured.

Ann had opened the window shields.

The view was clear, distance and debris all the way out to the stars—and the towering broken wall of the *Sky Rider* to one side. But it was not the death of the *Sky Rider* that held their eyes, and it was not the death of their own families they thought about—it was their own. A planet lay in their path. Orange, vermillion, ochre yellow and rusty brown—the atmosphere swirled. Small moons revolved around it and the great red spot glowed at them like a crimson eye.

"Jupiter," Glyn said grimly.

"We're heading straight for it!" Sonja cried.

"What's Joobitoo?" Caroline asked.

Matthew lifted her up.

It was not so terrible, not yet, just a world suspended in space and not much bigger than a golf ball. But it seemed to grow even as they watched it. Soon it would fill the sky, gigantic and deadly. Those raging belts of colors and clouds would drag them down and dash them to pieces on the unseen surface. Faced with that prospect, time regained its meaning. Second by second it was running out.

"Is we going to Joobitoo?" Caroline asked innocently.

"No!" Sonja said harshly.

"Where are you going then, girlie?" Glyn asked her.

"We've got to *do* something!" Sonja said.

"Like what?" Glyn asked desperately. "A quick U-turn back to Earth? How we going to do it then? Where's the retro motors? Where's the reversed thrust? What's the trajectory heading? How are we going to undock? We know nothing about spaceships, do we? We don't know anything! None of us do!"

But Ann sat in the control seat with her hand on a switch. Very still she was sitting, unspeaking, unmoving, frozen in midaction. And just like that Glyn had seen her in the moment he entered the cabin—her hand in the flame, her fingers poised just as they were now, exactly, as if she had known what she was about to do but had instantly forgotten. Glyn stared.

"Maybe if we throw that switch . . . ?" Glyn said.

"Do you think that's wise?" Matthew said.

It was not wise.

It was a kind of instinct.

"It could kill us!" Sonja said fearfully.

"Does it matter?" Glyn asked.

"I guess not," Matthew said quietly.

"You can't do it!" Sonja cried. "You can't! You can't!"

"Is Glyn going to kill me?" Caroline whimpered.

"No," said Matthew. "Of course he isn't."

But Glyn had to do something.

He had to know what that switch was for.

Quietly, so as not to alarm her, he knelt beside Ann's chair.

"Listen to me, girlie," Glyn said desperately. "I know I hurt you last night and I'm sorry for it, but I ain't going to hurt you now. You got to help us, see? You got to tell us what that switch is for. You hearing me, Ann?"

She turned her head.

He was crouched on his heels beside her. His eyes were gray as the hills of Wales she had once visited with her father, and in the hushed light they were all watching her, all waiting for an answer. Matthew held Caroline in his arms and slow tears rolled down Sonja's face. Ann struggled to remember. The ship was opened onto space and stars and the planet lay ahead of them. They had needed to know that, so the music had shown them—but now it was gone. Her hand was on the switch and she knew nothing. Blue fear showed in her eyes.

"No," said Glyn. "No, don't think about it. Just feel it, see? You know what it's for. You *do* know. If it's right you've got to press it, see?"

Ann bit her lip.

The knowledge was gone. Or maybe she had never known. She closed her eyes. She knew what Glyn asked and deep inside was a strange prompting—his voice in her mind saying, "Do it—do it!" And Sonja was screaming, "Don't touch! Don't touch it!" But Ann had to choose and then it was too late. She clicked the switch and a huge static crackle filled the cabin. A video screen flickered on—blank gray, fluctuating, waiting for contact. And next to it the frequency selector lit up, glowed green with its black numerals. Sonja's tears turned to laughter. In the barrage of noise she was wild and dancing as Matthew smiled and Caroline slipped from his arms to join her. Ann had found the radio.

In sheer relief Glyn put his arms around her. "Oh girlie," Glyn said. "I really do love you."

10

It was 3:25 by the control-cabin clock. Matthew glanced at his watch. Earth time said ten minutes past midnight. It was madness to stay awake. They could not take another twenty-hour day. Their whole sleeping-waking process was being thrown into disruption. White light beat on Matthew's eyes and the cabin seemed charged with an electrical quality, tensing his nerves like high-voltage cables, and even if he had tried he could not have slept then. There was too much excitement. Caroline jumped up and down, swung on Sonja's arm and wanted her to dance again. But all Sonja could think of was the radio. She gazed at it like a love object, oblivious of all else. And Ann sat passively in the chair, blue eyes watching Glyn, the movements of his hands, the moods on his face, his quiet muttering.

"Hurry up!" Sonja urge him.

"I got to find out how it works, haven't I?" Glyn retorted.

Now that Ann had singled out the radio from among all the other control panels, it was easy enough to understand. It was a video transceiver with a simple on-off switch and a row of knobs beneath the speaker. One by one Glyn tested them—frequency selector, volume control, sound pitch, receive and transmit. There were focal depth and brightness controls for the video screen and a knob labeled COMP which seemed to make no difference to anything.

"Let me have a go," Sonja said impatiently.

"And me! And me!" Caroline shrilled.

She reached for the controls she could not quite see.

The static roared as she turned up the volume.

"Let it alone!" Glyn said. "If you touch any of them switches again I'll clobber you! And I don't need any help from you either," he said to Sonja.

"I think you should go to bed, Caroline," Matthew murmured.

"No," said Caroline.

Matthew sighed.

"Then will you come over here please, out of Glyn's way?"

He moved away to sit on the floor by the door with his legs stretched out before him and patted the ground beside him for Caroline to join him. But she played a game with him instead, jumping backward and forward across his legs. Air from the vents was warm and sleepy. Shrill whistles came from the radio. Her footsteps thudded.

"Will you shut her up?" Glyn said.

"We can't hear a thing," said Sonja.

"Will you come and sit down, Caroline," Matthew told her.

"I'm jumping," Caroline informed him.

He caught her, held her head between her knees and playfully smacked her bottom. Her laughter stayed muffled as infinitely slowly, with Sonja breathing down his neck, Glyn changed frequencies. They listened for voices—human voices that were never there among the variations of cosmic noise. Through every frequency and back again the selector moved and they listened—but they heard nothing.

"Try transmitting," Matthew suggested.

Caroline squirmed from his grasp. "I want to see. You lift me up," she said to Sonja.

"There's nothing to see," Sonja told her.

"I want to look at the little television."

She clambered onto Ann's lap.

The control knobs were within her grasp. She reached to touch.

"Leave 'em alone!" Glyn shouted. "How many more times!"

Caroline retreated, went back to Matthew and sat beside him on the floor. Glyn had told her off. Her face was sulky and her thumb was in her mouth. Or perhaps she sensed the next few moments were important. She watched and scowled as the silence grew tense and filled the cabin. Glyn was about to transmit.

Receive and transmit—it was simultaneous. He cleared his throat, shifted the frequency. Static roared and he dulled his volume.

"Mayday. Mayday," Glyn said. "This is Life Ferry B. Are you reading me? Come in please. Over and out." Nothing happened and he tried again. "Mayday. Mayday. This is Life Ferry B. Can anyone hear us? We need help please. Over and out." Again nothing happened.

"Try another frequency," Sonja suggested.

Glyn altered the selector.

The static changed tone and dropped to a whisper.

"This is Life Ferry B. Is there anyone listening? Come in please. Mayday. Mayday. You got to help us. Over and out."

No one answered.

For hour after hour they listened and waited. Glyn's voice grew husky but he would not give up. He went on calling, doggedly repeating the same words over and over again as the frequencies shifted and the selector clicked through its numbers. And every shift brought a new hope, a new disappointment. Caroline grew restless, wandered around the cabin, then ran races with herself in endless circles. The thud of her feet and the soft airplane noises she made grew monotonous, as monotonous as the sound of Sonja's voice telling her to shut up and keep still. Matthew's face turned gray with tiredness. His eyelids drooped and his shirt stank of sour milk and Benjamin's piddle.

"Mayday! Mayday! This is Life Ferry B. We need your assistance. Come in please. Come in. Over and out."

The static crackled, changed to a whistle, screamed and faded and crackled again. Among a monotone of words and sounds the soft interferences sighed like the sea on a pebbly beach. And when Glyn finally switched off, the sound was still going on in Matthew's head—footsteps and airplanes and static noise that gradually faded into silence. The bang of Glyn's fist jolted him awake.

"What's wrong with the blasted thing?"

"You couldn't have got it switched on right," Sonja said.

"Okay, Marconi—if you're so clever, you take over!"

"All right! I will!"

Glyn gave up his seat and Sonja took it.

And Caroline tripped over Matthew's feet.

"Get that brat out of here!" Glyn said.

"I'm not a brat! I'm not a brat!" Caroline screamed.

"So how about going to bed?" Matthew suggested.

"I don't want to go to bed! I want to talk on the radio! I don't like you no more, Mattoo!"

"Ditto," Matthew said shortly.

"I've done enough anyway," Glyn said. "I got to get some sleep even if she don't need it."

"You can't leave the radio!" Sonja protested.

"Why not?" said Glyn. "I thought you were taking over."

"You can't leave me here on my own! What if someone answers?"

"In that case you got permission to wake me. Coming, girlie?" Glyn said to Ann.

She smiled and nodded and he held out his hand.

"It's not fair!" Sonja said.

"I can talk on the radio," Caroline muttered.

She was standing by the control panel in the

far corner of the cabin and all knobs were the same. "Mayday! Mayday!" Caroline said. She stood on tiptoe and her small fingers reached and grasped. But someone grabbed her arm. A hard hand landed several smacks around her naked legs and her screams were louder than Matthew's voice.

"When you're told to leave things alone," Matthew shouted, "you leave them alone! Understand? And now you're going to bed whether you like it or not!"

Much too soon for Matthew the day began again—the blue light turned to white and Benjamin awoke. But it was not Benjamin who made him feel desperate through the dragged-out time while Glyn and Sonja took turns on the radio and Jupiter grew nearer. Now that the measles rash had cleared away Benjamin demanded nothing but a change of diaper and an occasional feed. An angel baby with his gurgling smile, he sat on a space of floor in the middle of the gangway and played with his toys—all the things that had once belonged to Eleanor, the bell rattle and the building bricks, and a string of Sonja's beads. Everything put within his reach he would grasp with his fat little fist, examine intently and sample for taste. Benjamin was no trouble. It was Caroline who drove Matthew mad.

She drove him mad with her noise and her meddling, her sulks and whimpering and screaming fits of temper. It was a form of erosion, a wearing down of his better nature. Between himself and the others Caroline was a continual source of contention. He got sick of Glyn shouting at her, sick of hearing Sonja order her out of the control cabin and sick of Ann's bungling attempts to help. Her meekness made things worse. She became an outlet for Caroline's aggression, a target for her rudeness. Matthew wanted to shout that she was useless and tell her to go away—go and join Glyn and Sonja in the control cabin. But she was useless there too. Matthew was stuck with her, a scared rabbit, incapable of acting on her own initiative, incapable of standing up for herself. Give Matthew a hand with them kids, Glyn had told her, so she did, but she had no idea how. Nervously she picked up Uggy from the floor where Caroline had thrown him and offered him back. But Caroline threw him away again.

"Don't want him!" Caroline said, and kicked Ann on the shin.

Matthew slapped her.

"Don't ever let me see you kick Ann again!" Matthew told her. "And you must be stupid to sit there and let her do it!" he said to Ann.

Her eyes turned watery. She went to the

washroom and Matthew supposed she was crying. He did not have time to feel sorry. He was out of sympathy and out of patience and he had Caroline to contend with. "You're not to smack me, Mattoo!" Caroline screeched and hit him on the arm. He tried to ignore her. He went to the control cabin but she followed him, her voice screaming in rage and indignation. "You're not to smack me, I said! I shall tell Mummy on you!"

Nothing changed.

"This is Life Ferry B calling anyone," Glyn said. "We need help. Repeat—we need help. Come in please. Over and out. And get her out of here!" he said to Matthew.

Sonja shifted the wavelength.

"Why can't you keep her down the other end of the ship?"

"Why don't you?" Matthew said bitterly.

"You're the official nursemaid, boyo," Glyn said.

"Not anymore," said Matthew. "I've just resigned. You two can take over for a while."

"No!" shrieked Caroline. "I don't like them, Mattoo! I only like you! And you mustn't smack me no more! I shall tell Mummy! You pick me up! I want to be picked up!"

Caroline stamped her feet and roared in temper. Her clenched fists pummeled his thigh.

But he stood like a stone as Glyn swiveled around in the chair to face him.

"You can't resign, boyo," Glyn said desperately.

"I can't cope anymore," Matthew told him.

"You got Ann."

"Ann is sniveling in the washroom."

"We can't possibly have her in here," Sonja said.

"This is priority," said Glyn. "We got to get help, see?"

Matthew saw.

Jupiter hung the size of a blood orange directly ahead of them and they had no intention of having Caroline. He watched as Glyn spread his hands and turned back to the radio. He saw the smug pity in Sonja's smile, responsible for nothing. "Mayday! Mayday!" Glyn said.

Pushing Caroline ahead of him, Matthew returned to the main cabin, and the madness was inside him, building up, being added to. He did not even notice—Benjamin had shuffled on his bottom and reached for Uggy. He was sitting quite happily sucking the blue hairy ear, until Caroline saw. "Mine!" Caroline said angrily, and snatched Uggy away. Benjamin toppled. One blue ear came off in his hand. He banged his head on the floor and cried pitifully.

Caroline howled.

"Benjamin's broken Uggy, Mattoo!"

"Serves you right!" Matthew said heartlessly.

Gently he picked up the baby. He sat on the edge of the seat, rubbed the sore place on his head, extracted the ear from his fist and the fur from his mouth and quietly rocked him. Furiously Caroline screamed and hated him. Benjamin had broken Uggy but Matthew nursed him and kissed him and an unyielding forearm kept her at bay. He would not let her sit on his lap. He would not let her reach him. Into his blue stained shirt and the flesh beneath it Caroline sank her teeth. Terrible and cold was Matthew's face when he looked at her. And cold and terrible was his voice.

"Get away from me!" Matthew told her. "Get away and stay away before I really hurt you. Do you understand that? Get out of my sight and leave me alone!"

Caroline understood.

She went and sat in the seat by the space suits and it was different tears that she cried. Matthew bent his head. He wanted to cry too. He wanted to cry because everyone was dead and he was left alone. He was alone with Caroline, trapped in the light, and he could not escape. There was no world, no woods, no quietness of birdsong and butterflies—just a shine of light on ceilings and floors and walls, empty seats and the voices calling—Mayday! Mayday! This is Life

Ferry B. We need help please. We need help. But there was no one willing to help Matthew. No one willing to listen and understand.

He did not know how long he sat there, rocking the baby, thinking of nothing, seeing nothing but the glazed surfaces, silver, green and white. And the voices went on, monotone words that did not disturb the silence that surrounded him. His movements soothed, the constant rocking, backward and forward, like the swell of the sea against a cliff edge of mind. He could feel himself slipping away, drugged by tiredness—but some tiny part of him stayed alert and knowing. It was too quiet. Too peaceful. With a child like Caroline something had to be wrong.

He looked around. He hoped she had fallen asleep but he saw her squatting beside the air-lock door, and on the floor by her feet was a small plastic container. For two or three minutes Matthew watched her before things connected up. She had found the chrysalids and one by one she was posting them through the grill of the air vent. Ruthless and violent the anger rose inside him. He dumped Benjamin on the seat and he did not stop to reason.

She was only a child but from a great height Matthew descended upon her. She did not know why he hit her, she only knew he did. Again and again the flat of his hand struck her around her

112

legs and buttocks. He was wild and uncontrolled, shouting at her, maddened words which she could not understand. Destruction—life—butterflies— the succession of nouns was drowned in her sound and she screamed in terror and pain. Glyn came running, howling at Matthew to stop it, but he could not, would not stop. He went on hitting and hitting her until Sonja dragged her away and Glyn knocked him to the ground, knelt on top of him and forced his arm upward behind his back. Ann watched from the washroom doorway but Caroline did not want to look or see. She buried her face in Sonja's sweater and cried bitterly.

"I'll kill her!" Matthew screamed. "I'll kill her! I'll . . ."

Glyn applied the pressure.

"You want I should break your arm, boyo?"

Matthew groaned.

"Oh God—you're hurting me! Let go! Please!"

"Mattoo's hurting," Caroline wept. "Mattoo's hurting, Sonja!"

"Make them stop it!" Sonja said to Ann.

"Stop it!" Ann said. "Stop it! Stop it!" She pulled at Glyn's jacket. "Let him go!"

Glyn released him and stood back.

"Leave that kid alone!" Glyn said.

Matthew sat up.

In the quiet aftermath they were all watching him, strained faces in the light, eyes blank with shock. Even now they could not believe it, not of him. He rested his head on his knees and rubbed his shoulder where Glyn had wrenched it. He heard Caroline sobbing. He knew the meaning of shame. He had warned them, told them what would happen. They should have listened. They should have helped him, but now they watched him and accused.

"She's a kid," said Glyn. "She's just a kid. Why'd you do it? Why? You could have killed her!"

"She killed my butterflies," Matthew murmured.

"Your what?"

"Butterflies."

"What butterflies?" Sonja asked. "What's he talking about?"

"He's off his head," said Glyn. "Flaming bananas!"

Ann picked up the box.

One brown cocoon lay on a bed of cotton.

"I think he means this," Ann said.

Glyn stared at the thing Ann had given him.

He could not believe it.

"You'd beat up a four-year-old kid for a miserable cocoon?"

He hurled it across the cabin.

"It's a butterfly," Matthew said. "A living butterfly!"

But Benjamin fell off the seat and butterflies did not matter anymore. "See to that baby!" Glyn said. And Ann did not stop to think about it. She picked him up. In the past, when she had been forced to hold him, she had turned rigid with fear, her whole being shrank away from him. But this time was different. She forgot about herself. Benjamin was hurt and screaming, and all her reluctance dissolved in the need to comfort him. She held him close to her, soothed and talked to him and stroked his fine thistledown hair. He screamed louder, struggled to be free of her unfamiliar arms.

Matthew got shakily to his feet. "I'll take him."

"Like hell you will!" Glyn said.

"I'm quite capable," Matthew said.

"Yes," said Glyn. "And we know what you're capable *of*! Get him out of here," he said to Ann. "And her!" he told Sonja.

"No," Caroline whimpered. "I don't want to!"

"She's not my responsibility," Sonja said. Ann left.

There was violence lingering in the light between the three of them and she carried Benjamin through to the control cabin. She sat in one

115

of the silver chairs and cradled him against her breast, rocked him and consoled him, her soft words murmuring. And gradually he stopped struggling and his crying subsided. His tears dried and he twisted to look about him, bright eyes alert and interested.

"Hello Benjamin," Ann said.

At the sound of his name Benjamin turned to look at her, his blue baby stare fixed on her face, intent and curious. It was as if he were seeing her for the first time. His small perfectly formed fingers played with hers, flexed and gripped. And finally he smiled, a beautiful smile full of warmth and affection. Soft sounds gurgled in his throat. He was talking to her, a secret language only she could understand. His baby magic cast a spell. Feelings stirred inside her, a mixture of awe and love.

"Why didn't you tell me before?" Ann asked. "Why didn't you tell me you were beautiful?"

She laughed and hugged him. She was not alone anymore. Angry voices shouted in the main cabin, loud and hating, but Ann had Benjamin to love.

11

Winds of two hundred miles an hour swept across the surface of Jupiter. No successful scientific probe had ever landed there. No spaceship ever would. The men on Ganymede could only guess what it looked like, a landscape of shifting pack ice below the lethal atmosphere. Magnetic fluctuations, electrical storms and shifting sources of radiation fouled up their instrument readings. Swirling clouds obscured the visual features, although sometimes, when the clouds shifted and parted, they had brief glimpses of narrow streaks of underlying darkness and bright areas of light, enigmatic undertones which they could not explain away. After twelve years of research the giant planet remained uncharted, a dangerous mysterious world that filled the sky like a challenge. Only Mackenzie dared to approach it.

The control room was tense and quiet. The computers whirred, tireless machines receiving and analyzing information. Video screens filled one whole wall, television monitors showing belting clouds, Mackenzie's face and the survey ship, small as an insect, that hurtled downward, banked and straightened and skimmed along the upper atmosphere. Joe adjusted the radio transceiver. Relevant data flickered on a screen in front of him and Mackenzie's voice crackled over the main speakers.

"Altitude two thousand miles."

"Copy," said Joe.

"Speed one hundred ninety-six m.p.s."

"Copy."

"Returning for a second run."

"Will follow."

"Dropping to fifteen hundred miles."

"Good luck, Mac."

"Who needs luck, daddy-o?"

Static hissed as Mackenzie hit the clouds.

"The man's a maniac," Anton said.

"And the Devil looks after his own," Frobisher replied.

It was an insane confidence Mackenzie possessed, a kind of genius. He had scared the hell out of Joe on more than one occasion. And on more than one occasion Frobisher had placed him on report. Ignoring direct orders, gross insubordination, mishandling a spacecraft, blatant disregard for official procedure—the list of Mackenzie's shortcomings grew almost daily. It was as if he lived for the sole purpose of risking his life. Now he was set for the lowest pass ever over Jupiter. Dark fins showed briefly among sulfurous clouds. The turbulence struck him. Images turned to fuzz and his voice was drowned in a roar of static. But with Mackenzie in control of the ship, Joe had learned not to worry. Along with the rest of the men at Ganymede Base he was watching the main video screens for a break in the atmosphere.

"Parallel north fifty-three," someone called.

"Visibility four point one five and clearing."

"There," said Anton. "What's that?"

A dark linear streak showed on the left-hand screen.

"Cloud coloration," said Frobisher.

"It's a fissure, sir," someone informed him.

"It can't be," said Anton. "Look at the size of it!"

"Registering zero momentum, sir."

"We reckon it's some kind of ground feature."

But the clouds covered it before it was confirmed.

And the machines whirred on, checking and rechecking.

Frobisher nodded.

"Tell Mackenzie I want another look at it," he told Joe.

"Mac?" said Joe. "Are you receiving me?"

There was no answer.

"This is Ganymede Base calling Survey Two Three. Do you read me, Mackenzie? Come in please."

Almost immediately the ship rose clear of the atmosphere.

Mackenzie's face returned to the screen.

"Oh boy! That was better than a roller coaster ride."

"In that case," said Joe, "you won't mind making another pass."

"Sure thing," Mackenzie said.

"Parallel north fifty-three—a straight run."

"Will go, Joe," Mackenzie sang out. "I'll give you a real close look this time. Dropping to one thousand miles."

"No way!" Anton said. "That's too risky!"

"You can't do it, Mac," Joe said.

"You want to bet?" Mackenzie asked him.

The ship turned, hurtled down toward the clouds.

"Stop him!" Frobisher ordered.

"You're no go, Mackenzie," Joe said quickly. "No go at one thousand miles. Repeat—no go. And that's an order!"

But Mackenzie was already gone.

Caroline knelt in the silver chair next to Ann. Light in the cabin gleamed gold on her hair, glinted on the massed controls and the switched-off radio. One by one she touched the scarlet buttons. No one told her not to. Sonja was sitting where Matthew had sat the night before—on the floor with her back to the wall. She wore an expression of annoyance on her face. "We got to look after them kids for a bit," Glyn had told her. But it was Sonja who got landed with Caroline, not him. She had to keep Caroline in the control cabin out of Matthew's way.

"It's all right for him!" Sonja said angrily.

"Why?" said Ann.

"He just gives the orders. We're the ones who have to do things."

Ann jigged Benjamin on her lap.

"You're not doing anything," Ann pointed out.

"I should have known you'd take his side!" Sonja snapped.

"I'm not taking anyone's side."

"You could have fooled me! You think you're something special just because you found the radio! But I've been calling since four o'clock last night without a thank you!"

"I can talk on the radio," Caroline offered hopefully.

"You let it alone!" Sonja told her.

"I want to," Caroline said tearfully.

And Ann made the decision.

With Benjamin trapped under the arch of her body she leaned forward and switched on. Static blared and she lowered the volume.

"Go ahead," Ann said to Caroline.

"You can't let her do that!" Sonja said furiously.

"Why not?" Ann asked. "Does it matter who transmits as long as someone does? I expect she can do it as well as you can."

Mackenzie had been missing for twelve minutes. A blast of sonic whistling came from the speakers and nothing showed on the video screens but wavering lines. Whatever information his instruments might be transmitting did not reach Ganymede, and their instruments failed to penetrate the depth of the atmosphere and locate him. They knew, if Mackenzie was down there, there was nothing they could do anyway, yet they were bound to try and Frobisher spared no effort.

122

All the main tracking systems were operational. Regular frequency channels were opened and monitored. They had set up a computer trace based on the last known coordinates, and outside on the launch pad a second survey ship was ready to take off. The room was a chaos of activity, men and movement, but beneath the headphones Joe was isolated. He worked alone, a senior radio operator conducting a full radio search.

"This is Ganymede Base calling Survey Two Three. Come in, Survey Two Three. Do you read me, Mackenzie? Come in please." Sweat beaded his forehead under the hot light. He shifted the frequency. "This is Ganymede Base calling Survey Two Three. Are you receiving me? Come in, Mackenzie. Over."

He knew, even as he spoke, that he was way out of Mackenzie's range, sweeping the empty distances of space out toward the orbit of Saturn, in toward the orbits of the asteroids. He knew Mackenzie could not be there. Speed and time made it impossible. He heard what he expected to hear—shifts of static varying only in pitch and tone. Then suddenly, amid the solar crackle, he heard a voice.

"Mayday! Mayday! We is Life Ferry P calling anybody. Is you listening someone? Help urgent please. Come over, I said."

Joe listened.

The message was repeated.

A young child called for assistance.

Caroline talked on the radio.

"And a fat lot of good that's going to do us," Sonja said sourly.

"She's happy, isn't she?" Ann retorted.

"She's just wasting time! There's no point in transmitting without changing channels. She should be moving the wavelength control."

"Why don't you stop criticizing and leave her alone?"

"Glyn told *me* to work that radio!"

"I thought you weren't taking any more orders from Glyn."

"I'm not."

"So shut up then, and let Caroline get on with it."

Sonja raised her eyebrows.

Something was different about Ann. She was not dumb and scared anymore, afraid to open her mouth. She had broken up a fight between Glyn and Matthew, answered Sonja back and stood up for Caroline. Static screamed and softened as Caroline altered the volume. And her voice went on, repeating the words she had heard.

"This is Life Ferry P. We is needing help urgent, somebody. You listen. I'm telling you come in. Over."

124

"You're not even saying it right," Sonja said scornfully.

"I am!" said Caroline. "I am saying it right!"

"It's not P. It's B. B for Butterfly."

Caroline pouted.

Next to her Benjamin jigged and laughed. His diaper was weighted down with wetness and his strong legs dug into Ann's lap. He was trying to stand, leaning forward to reach the radio controls. Caroline pushed his hand away.

"I'm doing it, Benjamin! Not you! We is B for Butt'fly calling someone. . . ."

Joe removed the headphones.

"Get Frobisher," he said to Anton.

"You've found Mac?"

"Never mind Mackenzie. Just get Frobisher."

Anton caught the urgency in Joe's voice. There was no time to ask questions. Over the nearest intercom Anton relayed the message. "Mr. Frobisher to radio control, please. Mr. Frobisher to radio control." In the vast lower spaces of the room men turned their heads and looked toward him. He could feel the questioning of dozens of pairs of eyes.

"What's going on?" Frobisher asked.

Joe was back beneath the headphones.

Anton tapped him on the shoulder.

"Frobisher," he mouthed.

"What's going on?" Frobisher repeated.

"I want a standby silence, a full transceiver linkup and a positive computer fix," Joe told him.

There was a long pause.

Nothing changed in Frobisher's face. Joe was asking for precedence over Mackenzie's life and he did not need to question the importance. Without a word he nodded and turned away. Over the internal speakers Frobisher barked his orders and was obeyed. All movement ceased. The machines whirred on but the men maintained a waiting silence. Mackenzie was left to face the consequences of his own actions and the room belonged to Joe.

"Go ahead," Frobisher said curtly.

Joe completed the switch through.

It was a child who spoke, a very young child.

Her little girl's voice was loud in the hushed room.

"Mayday! Mayday!" she said angrily. "We is B for Butt'fly calling someone. Why isn't you listening? Help urgent, I said. You answer me!"

Stunned faces of men stayed motionless in the light.

Even Frobisher stood transfixed.

"I don't believe it," Anton said softly.

"Mayday! Mayday!" the child repeated. "We is B for Butt'fly calling someone. Is you listening?

Help urgent, please. Over and come in. You answer—damn hell!"

Joe did not wait for the order.

He flicked the transmission switch.

"I answer," Joe said calmly. "This is Ganymede Base. What can we do for you, *Butterfly*?"

There was nothing Glyn could do. The lock was red on the washroom door and Matthew refused to open it. He shrugged and went to the control cabin. Sonja was sitting on the floor and Caroline talked over the radio.

"Who said she could do that?" Glyn asked angrily.

"*She* did," Sonja told him.

Ann swung around in the chair to face him and Glyn changed his attitude. There was quietness in her eyes, blue calm like summer skies. They were all going crazy, feeling desperate and falling apart, but Ann knew what she was doing.

"Keeping her quiet, are you girlie?" Glyn said respectfully. "How's that baby?"

She smiled down at Benjamin on her lap.

"He's beautiful," she said simply. "But his diaper's soaking."

"Go and get a clean one," Glyn told Sonja.

"Get one yourself!" Sonja said mutinously.

"You answer—somebody!" Caroline told the radio.

She turned up the volume.

The static screamed and crackled.

Then a man's voice came from the speakers, deafeningly loud.

"I answer," said the man. "This is Ganymede Base. What can we do for you, *Butterfly*?"

Caroline recoiled in fright but Sonja leaped to her feet. Her eyes shone. The anger left her face. It was as if the whole universe full of hope and glory was contained in that man's voice. She forgot she hated Glyn. She let out a whoop of joy and flung her arms around his neck. Half laughing, half crying, she swung him around.

"They're answering! They're answering! Did you hear?"

"I ain't deaf," Glyn said.

"We're saved! We're saved!"

"Lemme get to that radio!"

"It's a man," said Caroline. "He spoked to me."

"So shift out the way," Glyn said, "and let me come there!"

Caroline scrambled to the floor and Ann left her seat. Carrying Benjamin, she took Caroline by the hand and led her out of the control cabin. Sonja spun in ecstatic circles, and seated in Caroline's chair Glyn lowered the volume.

"Answer him! Answer him!" Sonja said.

"This is Life Ferry B," said Glyn. "B for Butterfly calling Ganymede Base. You got to help us, mister. There's been an accident, see? We're on our own and heading straight for Jupiter and I don't know how to drive this thing. Come in please. Over and out."

12

The men listened and waited. There was nothing they could do until the child responded. But she went on calling, her dictatorial tones repeating the same message. "You answer—damn hell!" Joe felt tempted to transmit again but he too was bound to maintain the silence. And suddenly the child stopped. Different voices were heard in the background, shouts and laughter and the thud of feet, as if someone were holding a party.

"It's a joke," said Anton. "It's got to be a joke."

But it was no joke.

The child was gone and a boy took over, a boy with a Welsh accent, young and unqualified. Joe caught the desperation in his voice. There had been an accident, he said. And the standby was over. Trained men moved into action. Computer readouts were analyzed and the relevant data transferred to the small screen on Joe's control panel.

Frobisher leaned over his shoulder.

"What do we have?"

"Not a lot," Joe said.

"No visual contact. No computer contact. And a twelve-point-four-five-minute time lag."

"Get rid of the time lag first?" Joe asked.

"I think so," Frobisher agreed.

Joe flicked the transmission switch.

"He's not answering," Sonja said.

Glyn tried again.

"This is Life Ferry B—B for Butterfly . . . calling Ganymede Base. . . ."

Still the man did not answer.

"Where the hell's he got to?" Glyn said.

Minutes went by.

"He's not answering," Sonja said again.

"Tell me something I don't know," Glyn snapped.

"You can't have done it right."

"It's switched on, isn't it?"

"So why isn't he answering?"

"Try asking a radio engineer."

"You must have shifted the frequency."

"I never touched it!"

"She did then! That blasted Caroline! She shifted it! I bet she did!"

"If she did, we've had it," Glyn said grimly.

"I'll go and get her," Sonja said.

"What for? She won't remember, she's just a kid."

"But he was *there*!" Sonja said brokenly. "He spoke to her. We heard him. We can't lose him now! We can't! He's the only one who can help us!"

She stared at the clock above the doorway. Red digital seconds clicked away. Ten minutes had passed, maybe more . . . she could not keep track of that kind of time. Fear and anger were growing inside her and their chances were slipping away as Glyn drummed his fingers on the chair arm.

"I don't understand," Glyn said.

"There's got to be something we can do!" Sonja exploded. "Try moving the frequency selector."

She reached out to touch the switch.

But Glyn gripped her hand.

"Don't touch it!"

"Why not?"

"Because he's there! He's got to be there!"

"But he isn't!" Sonja screamed. "He isn't answering!"

"This is Life Ferry B," said Glyn. "Calling Ganymede Base. You've got to hear us, mister. You've got to answer. For pity's sake . . . answer!"

But only the static answered, soft and whispering.

And the silences behind it.

"I can't bear it," Sonja wept.

Glyn leaned back in the chair.

His face was bitter.

Gray depression grew in his eyes.

Sonja sniffed and gnawed her fingernails. He had nothing to say to her, no way to comfort. Tick, tick . . . the digital seconds counted away his life. He could not bear it either. He was beaten. Minute by minute the giant planet drew nearer and what Glyn faced was the inevitability of death. Then, once again, the radio crackled.

"This is Ganymede Base," the man said. "Receiving you loud and clear, *Butterfly*. But we have a twelve-minute-plus time lag between messages. Will you switch your radio through to the on-board computer, please. Repeat . . . will you please press the computer button on your radio control panel."

And Sonja was not crying anymore.

Her eyes shone.

"There!" Sonja said. "Hurry up!"

Glyn pressed the computer button.

"I've done that, mister."

The reply was immediate now.

"Copy, *Butterfly*. We have zero delay. We are standing by for a video link-up."

"What's a video link-up?" Glyn asked.

"The telescreen," Sonja said quickly.

"You should find the controls to the right of your radio transceiver and below the video screen," said the man.

Glyn switched on.

The small screen brightened as it had done once before. But now the blank gray flickered with color and he could see the blurred outline of a face. He adjusted the focus and the man came clear. It was a pleasant face with brown hair and a beard. And his gray eyes seemed to stare directly at Glyn and Sonja. He was perhaps in his mid-thirties.

"I'm Joe," he said.

What Joe saw on his own video screen was the cabin of the life ferry and two teenagers—a boy in a starship uniform and a girl with dark eyes brimming tears. He was not sure what he felt— surprise or alarm or a mixture of both—but Sonja gabbled her joy to see him. Her name was Sonja Rawlings, she said, and the boy's name was Glyn. They had been trapped for days, she said, and they had given up hope until he came. Joe nodded, smiled politely, and looked at Glyn.

"What happened?" he asked.

"There was an accident," Glyn said.

"What kind of accident?"

"We hit an asteroid, I guess."

"Who's we?"

"The *Sky Rider*."

"I see," Joe said briefly. "How many on board the life ferry?"

"Six," said Glyn. "Including Caroline and the baby."

"Just six?"

"Everyone else is dead."

"I see," Joe said again. "Who's in charge?"

"I am," said Glyn.

Joe's face showed no change of expression. He kept his voice calm.

"Excuse me for just a moment," Joe said.

He turned away.

And the mask dropped.

He was not just a radio operator—he was a man. His feelings showed then, an appalled mixture of horror and shock. He had to struggle to accept what he heard, struggle to believe. A communications breakdown, according to reports from Earth . . . but the *Sky Rider* had been hit by an asteroid. She carried more than a thousand persons and only six had survived. The extent of the tragedy overwhelmed him.

"Did you hear that?" Joe asked Frobisher.

"I heard," Frobisher affirmed.

"How do we handle it?"

"We can't," said Anton. "They're all kids, by the sound of it. That boy isn't capable of handling a spacecraft, not even with our help. We're simply not equipped to deal with a situation like this."

"And that's what I'm supposed to tell them, is it?" Joe asked. "Say we're very sorry but we're only here to study the Jovian climate, try somewhere else?"

Light shone on Frobisher's graying hair. He was the Base Controller and the decision was his. His still gray eyes betrayed nothing of the mind behind them, nothing of what he thought or felt. He had abandoned Mackenzie to his fate, but Joe knew he would not abandon a boy and a child and a baby. He listened as Anton reeled off the facts. They would need full details of *Butterfly*'s immediate situation—a complete computer read-out, her mass, her tonnage, her speed and her trajectory heading. They would need to compute course corrections, deceleration, orbital velocity and eventual landing procedure—none of which Glyn would be capable of carrying out.

"Which suggests we need to initiate a full computer transfer and pilot the ship from here," Frobisher said.

"Which is okay in theory," Anton said.

"We have enough qualified men."

"Sure," said Anton. "We can handle the computer side of it, but where's your qualified pilot? Johnson's competent enough at flying a survey tug, but *Butterfly*'s a different proposition altogether. She's fast."

"So is Mackenzie," Frobisher reminded him.

"And Mackenzie is missing," Anton said.

"You should keep in touch, my friend."

"You mean he's not missing?"

"Estimated time of arrival twenty hundred hours."

Anton frowned. "Are you prepared to trust Mackenzie?"

Joe knew the answer to that.

He turned back to the radio.

"Okay," Joe said. "We'll get you out of there. Don't worry."

137

13

Matthew sat on the washroom floor. It was a kind of prison. Blank walls and shut doors closed him in. He sat for a long time, doing nothing, staring at the floor. The lighting flickered. He heard water trickling through the recycling system—tiny tinkling sounds. Ann tried the door and called to him, but he did not move or answer and she went away. The cabin seemed a million miles away, another world he did not want to reenter and faces he did not want to see or know. He stayed where he was, locked in the watery quietness with all his guilt and shame. He knew what he had done. He had beaten Caroline. Slow tears spilled from his eyes. The sick feeling grew in his stomach and his thoughts punished him.

"You can do time for child battering," Glyn had said.

There was no anger now, no justification—just flickers of light on a green linoleum floor, just tinkling music. Tiredness and misery played games with his mind. Light and sound—the hallucinations troubled him. They grew wilder and wilder, flickering and chiming, washing his brain and draining him of feeling. The air flashed, gold and white, surrounding him with pale fire, and the music went on, a voice somewhere singing a wordless song. He was losing touch with reality, slipping away into some timeless existence, his mind cocooned in the music of a lullaby, a bright dream of unknowing, beautiful and kind. He heard the banging of fists on the door. He heard Sonja's voice.

"Are you going to be in there all day?"

But she could not disturb him.

Deeper he sank, deeper into the heart of music and light.

Wings of butterflies beat through his brain.

On Ganymede the room was hushed. The number-three video screen showed a blueprint layout of the controls of a standard life ferry, and the internal scanner, which Glyn had

139

switched on, showed it in actuality. It was imperative, said Frobisher, that they instigate a computer takeover immediately. There was no time for personal involvement. Joe had sent Sonja away, and only Glyn remained. Patterns of binary numbers appeared in groups on the telescreen and he read them over.

"Zero one, zero one, zero."

Glyn depressed the computer keys.

His face was intent with concentration.

He had already made one slipup and had to begin again.

"I got that," Glyn said.

"Copy," said Joe. "Double one, zero, double one."

"Double one . . . zero . . ."

Sonja returned to the control cabin.

"Matthew's locked in the washroom," Sonja said.

Glyn ignored her.

"Zero double one," he said to Joe. "Go on."

"He's locked in the washroom and he won't come out," Sonja said.

"Clear the computer," said Joe.

"Why?" said Glyn.

"Your readout shows one extra zero."

Quick and alarmed, Glyn turned his anger on Sonja.

"You great stupid cow! I lost it! All them

numbers! Double one blinking zero—and you fouled it up! You and your big mouth!"

"Cool it," said Joe.

"I thought you told her to stay out the way!"

"Just cool it!"

"It's not my fault!" Sonja said angrily. "I want to go!"

"You'll go!" said Glyn. "On the end of my toe!"

Joe swung around in his chair.

"We have a stress situation," he said urgently.

"I'll handle it," Frobisher said grimly.

Joe relinquished his seat.

Frobisher was used to handling human situations, the stress and distress of people in confined quarters. For five years he had maintained discipline on Ganymede. He could not intervene directly between Glyn and Sonja, or physically prevent the violence that simmered between them, but he could distract their attention. He switched off the transceiver. The video screens went dead and *Butterfly* was cut off. Static screamed in the cabin and everything ended.

Glyn let go of Sonja's arm.

Joe had abandoned them.

"Now look what you've done!" Glyn howled.

"It wasn't me," said Sonja. "It wasn't me!"

"Where's he gone, for God's sake?"

Glyn flicked the transceiver off and on.

"We've been cut off!" Glyn said.

"What'll we do?" Sonja said sickly.

They stared at the telescreen. Ahead of them the moons revolved around Jupiter, growing closer and larger even as they watched. Long blank minutes went by, and when the contact was restored it was not Joe who smiled at them. It was a gray-haired man with hard eyes and a steely expression. The silence was ominous.

"My name is Frobisher," the man said coldly. "I am the Base Controller. I do not tolerate disruptive behavior from my men and I will not tolerate it from you. Whatever personal problems you have must wait. You, young lady, will leave the control cabin and not return until you are told to do so. And you, boy, will complete the computer transfer which I shall dictate. Is that clear?"

Glyn swallowed nervously.

And Sonja turned to go.

Losing Joe was a kind of grief.

With Frobisher in command Glyn made no mistakes. He did not dare. His whole body was tense and sweating and his head ached with the effort, eyes and mind focused solely on what he did. There was nothing beyond it, only the voice that had to be obeyed, only the endless succession of numbers—zero one, zero double one, going

142

on and on. And then, suddenly, it was over.

"Well done, boy," Frobisher said kindly.

Glyn stared at him.

"You mean that's all there is to it?"

"That's all. The computer transfer is complete, and we have control of your ship. Now let's forget about the mechanics. According to the young lady there's some kind of problem. . . ."

"Yes," said Glyn. "I'm not sure what."

"I suggest you go and find out," Frobisher said. "And go easy—understand? If you're unsure how to handle it, report back. I appreciate the situation you're in and we have the base medic standing by. Good luck."

Glyn nodded.

On Ganymede things were starting to happen, but in the main cabin of *Butterfly* nothing had changed. The same harsh light shone on the same silver seats. The same atmosphere prevailed, moody and dangerous. Sonja leaned against the wall by the washroom door. Caroline was shouting for Matthew to come out and Benjamin cried irritably in Ann's arms, wanting his feed. Ganymede might have taken control of the ship, but they could not take over people. A locked door confronted Glyn, and the need to open it. He shouted and banged with his fists.

"Open up! Do you hear me? Come out of there!"

Matthew made no reply.

"He won't answer," Ann told him.

"If you don't come out, boyo," Glyn shouted, "I'm coming in!"

There was a glass panel beside the door.

EMERGENCY, it said. BREAK GLASS TO RELEASE DOOR.

Glyn did not hesitate. It was like an old habit—sleeve over fist, a quick smash and an automatic hiss. The door opened and Sonja pushed past him. Matthew lay in a collapsed heap on the floor, but she could not wait to see if he was dead or alive. The lock turned behind her on the toilet door and Glyn was left to find out. He stood looking down on him. His face was drained white, completely bloodless. Reflections of pale light played on his glasses and something hovered in the room behind him. Glyn spun around. There was nothing there, just Ann come to the doorway, her skirt fluttering in the heat from the air vent and the pale drifting of her hair.

"Is he all right?" Ann asked.

"I dunno," Glyn said.

Ann knelt beside him.

He was not dead, he was sleeping.

But she could not rouse him.

"I'll go and report back," Glyn said.

"Mattoo! Mattoo!" Caroline cried. "You wake up!"

Gently Ann slapped his face, and he opened his eyes. She was a girl calling him, golden amid light and part of the song in his head. But her face was blurred and her words were meaningless, lost in the music and part of the dream. Drugged colors shifted around him, soft and summery, green and golden and white, in a flush of water and a far off baby cry. "Mattoo! Mattoo!" Caroline shouted. And then Sonja was shaking him, a shadowy person slowly coming clear. Scarlet on black he saw the motif of the Galaxy Hunters emblazoned across her chest. He saw the darkness of her hair and eyes. He struggled to remember—wings of butterflies and a strange forgotten song.

Glyn gripped his arm.

"On your feet, boyo," Glyn said. "Get hold of him," he said to Sonja. "We got to get him to the control cabin, Joe said."

Anton was not much concerned with the human aspects of the situation, the transactions and interreactions of the people concerned, how Joe coped or what Frobisher and the doctor decided. On the vast lower-floor space of the control room Anton had a different job to do, the coordination of men and machines and the computerized functioning of *Butterfly*.

"Activate forward scanners," Anton said.

"Forward scanners on," came the reply.

"Full scan—one hundred eighty degrees."

"Commencing."

"Magnification six point five."

The men saw what had happened to the *Sky Rider*. The video screens showed it. Cameras panned across wreckage and stars. Bodies of people, fragments of hull, floated hundreds of miles out, impelled by the impact and diminishing into distance, revealed now by the focal power of the scanners. It was as if the whole ship had been blown apart. Nothing remained of it but a single deck and the rearing wall to which *Butterfly* was attached. Like the rest of the wreckage she was dragged by inertia along an uncontrolled trajectory that was vaguely directed toward Jupiter.

"Good grief," someone murmured.

But it was not feelings Anton wanted, it was facts.

"I want that trajectory heading," Anton said.

"Being computed," Jim Hayes told him.

"Closest approach to Jupiter?"

"Approximately six hundred thirty thousand miles."

"Present speed?"

"Eighteen hundred fifty-two miles per second."

"I think we have problems," Jim Hayes said.

They had problems.

146

Butterfly was going too fast. Like the *Sky Rider*, she was designed for interstellar travel, building up huge speeds across vast distances and needing vast distances to slow down. But there were only 107.5 million miles between her and Ganymede. They could not wait for Mackenzie to arrive. They would need to initiate undocking procedure and commence deceleration immediately. It was time to advise Frobisher.

"Check all systems go and remain on standby," Anton ordered.

"If you're going to see Frobisher," Jim Hayes said, "you had better inform him that we have an unidentified power source on board *Butterfly*."

"What?" said Anton.

The man pointed.

A tiny pulse of light showed on a small computer screen.

Matthew took off his glasses. His hands shook, his shirt was filthy and his hair was a mess. He looked like some kind of tramp. Joe studied his ashen face. He was no expert but he recognized fatigue when he saw it and he sensed that Matthew had reached the breaking point. It was not an easy thing to admit. Caroline had killed the butterflies and he could not take any more.

"So I hit her," Matthew said sickly.

"Because she killed the butterflies?"

147

"*Gonepteryx rhamni*," Matthew murmured. "Yellow brimstones."

"Cocoons," said Glyn. "He kept them in a box."

"Then what happened?" Joe asked.

"I hit *him*," Glyn said.

"You mean you knocked him out?"

"No," said Glyn. "He must have passed out—in the washroom."

"And that was when you heard music and thought you saw something?"

"Yes," said Matthew.

"But it ain't just him," said Glyn.

Joe nodded.

Glyn had seen it on two previous occasions and so had the girl, Ann. He turned to the doctor. The picture was coming clear. They were dealing with what appeared to be collective psychological disturbances, visual and auditory hallucinations, which was not uncommon among people confined together. A case of hypnotic suggestion, the consequences of stress, emotional and mental disorder.

"When did you last eat?" Joe asked.

"I can't remember," Matthew said.

"How about sleep?"

"Not much. Benjamin cried until past midnight and then Ann woke us. Three hours perhaps?"

148

"You realize you had a time discrepancy on board?"

"Three hours fifteen minutes."

"Is it morning or evening?"

"Pardon?"

"What day of the week is it?"

"Hang on a minute," Glyn said.

"How long ago did the accident happen?"

"Monday," said Glyn.

"That's not what I asked."

"If you just give us a chance to think . . ."

"Did you have relatives on board the *Sky Rider*?"

"Yes," said Matthew.

"Have you thought about what it means?"

"There doesn't seem much point in thinking about it."

"Have you taken a shower since you came aboard *Butterfly*?"

"What's that got to do with it?" Glyn asked.

"Have you cleaned your teeth or combed your hair?"

"What is this? A blasted inquisition?"

It was question and answer, a medical assessment, and they failed to keep track. They got more and more muddled. Everything that had happened was falling apart into a kind of mental chaos, disjointed rememberings of a series of incidents that had no sequence in time . . . a dead

149

man's face and a ball of light in an empty corridor, the scream of the window shields being opened, Uggy and Benjamin, Caroline and measles spots and no one in charge. The base doctor listened. It was not encouraging—suppressed shock experiences, sleep deprivation, lack of personal routine, disorientation, signs of emotional instability and perceptual distortions. It could not go on.

"Sedation?" Frobisher suggested.

The doctor nodded.

"At least twenty-four hours, I think."

Joe turned around.

"Sedation," Frobisher told him.

"Hypnodine thirty-four," the doctor said. "Two capsules each and one for the baby, split and administered in milk. They should have a standard emergency drug supply on board."

"Hypnodine thirty-four," Joe repeated. "Eleven capsules."

"Thirteen," said the doctor.

"Why thirteen?"

"Six persons and a baby."

"Six?" said Frobisher. "There are only five."

The doctor raised his eyebrows.

"Not according to the medical evidence of the computer. We are recording seven heartbeats, seven distinct brainwaves, and seven separate sources of life energy. So I conclude we have seven persons on board, including the child and the baby, of course."

150

Frobisher stared at him.

Something was wrong.

"Excuse me, sir," Anton said. "I think you should know we have an unidentified power source on board *Butterfly*."

Music and light, Matthew had said.

A ball of light in an empty corridor, Glyn had reported.

For Joe things connected up.

And a cold fear gripped his heart.

14

It was not a collective hallucination. It was actually there. On Ganymede the sensors showed it, shifting restlessly behind the walls—a bright pulse of light on a blueprint layout, beta waves on an electroencephalograph machine. As a natural phenomenon it was not unknown to them. They had heard rumors of it before, music and light along the corridors of Lunar Base before the main dome collapsed, reported on board a cargo tug before it blew up and logged by the explorers of the third Martian expedition who had afterward died in a freak sandstorm. It was a portent of disaster. And now it was aboard *But-*

152

terfly, established like a terrible omen, and recognized for what it really was—not a natural phenomenon at all, but an alien life form. The whole room seemed frozen out of action. Fear traveled like a contagion from man to man, and Frobisher changed his plans.

"I want that thing watched!" he said.

"Maintain full surveillance," Anton instructed.

"And keep those kids on the alert," Frobisher told Joe.

"Stimulants?" Joe said quietly.

The doctor shook his head. The alien presence posed no immediate threat to human life. The red alert was best confined to Ganymede, and there was no need to involve the occupants of *Butterfly*. And Joe gave nothing away. His voice stayed controlled and in his eyes there was no trace of alarm. He merely relayed the doctor's instructions.

"Go make yourselves a meal," he told Glyn and Matthew. "A full meal with twenty-five grams of glucose added to a glass of vitamin orange. Take a shower, clean yourselves up and the base doctor would like to see Caroline for a medical checkup."

She came with Sonja a few minutes later, a fair-haired little girl with a tousled ponytail. Joe had never handled a child before. He had nothing against them, but in a troubled universe he had long ago decided against the responsibility of fatherhood. Now, blue and fierce, Caroline's eyes were fixed on his face. He was the man who had spoken to her on the radio. His loud voice had scared her, and she had not been allowed in the control cabin since he had come. She did not like men with beards, and she refused to show him where the spots had been.

"I shall tell Glyn not to give you any pea soup," Sonja threatened.

"Don't want pea soup!" Caroline muttered.

"How about fetching Uggy to show me?" Joe suggested.

"Benjamin deaded him," Caroline said evilly.

"And you're not going to show me your spots?"

"No."

Caroline was difficult and defiant, but when Joe finally made the breakthrough he wished he had not. It was like being taken over. She showed him her tummy maybe twenty times, and twenty times he was forced to admire it, pale and spotless above a pair of pink panties. Her ceaseless flow of chatter blasted him out of thought. When she questioned him he had to answer, and when she gave an order he had to obey. She wanted to know if his beard was real, and when they arrived on Ganymede she wanted roast turkey and ice cream. He was a captive audience, and her voice grew shrill with excitement. Round and round she swung in the silver chair and commanded him to watch her. She was beyond control, a child on a knife edge. Hyperactive, the doctor murmured. This was the child who had driven Matthew to strike and it was not hard to understand why. Dark shadows ringed Sonja's eyes and what little patience she had was wearing thin.

"Will you stop swinging on that chair!" Sonja snapped.

"I can jump," said Caroline. "You watch me, Joe."

"Get down," Joe said. "Before you fall."

But she was too quick.

To the edge of the swinging chair she moved and balanced, her feet on the soft plastic, her hands raised with nothing to grip. And Sonja was slow to react. Caroline toppled, fell before she could stop her, struck her head on the radio panel and crashed to the floor. Her shrill screams echoed through the main speakers, filled the room on Ganymede; and a trickle of blood seeped from a cut on her forehead. Sonja panicked and rushed hysterically into the main cabin screaming that Caroline had cut her head open, and Joe was left to watch—a hurt crying child with millions of miles between them. Never before had he experienced such total helplessness.

"For pity's sake!" Joe said. "Someone see to that child!"

It was Matthew who came, picked Caroline up, rocked and consoled her and stanched the blood with a stained handkerchief. It was fright more than hurt caused the noise.

"Maybe now you'll behave yourself," Matthew said.

Joe repeated the doctor's orders.

"Get her fed. Give her one capsule of hypnodine thirty-four and put her to bed. She should sleep for at least twelve hours."

"I don't want to go to bed, Mattoo!" Caroline howled.

Matthew said nothing.

But into his eyes came a look of sheer relief.

There was one more interview to conduct.

"Sit down, sweetheart," Joe told her.

She sat in the chair with the baby in her arms—madonna in the light, flaxen haired and shy. He had to coax the words out of her. But gradually she lost her nervousness. Her voice grew stronger and she answered him clearly, dutifully, her blue eyes watching his face. Her name was Ann Trethowen, she said, and she had come from Devon in England. Like the others she could not remember when she had last eaten or slept, what day of the week it was or how long she had been there. But she remembered other things. She remembered the music when Joe questioned her.

It was a strange story she told—sleigh bells and icicles and prickles of gold, on board the *Sky Rider* and on *Butterfly*. She had seen a ball of dancing light that had changed into a pillar of flame. She claimed it had shown her how to close the air lock and where to find the radio. It was almost as if she and it had established some form of telepathic communication.

"It was trying to help," Ann said.

"Weren't you afraid of it?" Joe asked her.

She thought for a moment.

"Some things are so beautiful you have to be afraid of them," Ann admitted. "Like angels, or thunderstorms. Like him," she said as she touched the baby's tiny hand. "He was terrifying until I got to know him."

Joe knew what she meant.

An amalgamation of beauty and terror.

He felt that way about Jupiter.

"Well, it's obviously quite harmless, whatever it is," Joe said lightly. "Nothing to worry about anyway."

"I don't," Ann said certainly.

But Frobisher did not trust it.

Unlike Joe he could not pretend to dismiss it, nor could he take the word of an inexperienced girl. He had watched it too long on the blueprint layout, shifting and drifting through the air vents, moving between the power cables toward the main drive unit. It moved with a purpose, a chilling intention, building its legend of death and destruction. With human lives Frobisher could take no chances. The surveillance continued. Every wire, every circuit, every instrument, every switch had to be checked and rechecked until he was satisfied.

"Is there anything else you want to know?" Ann asked.

Joe shook his head.

He could learn nothing from Ann. She had too much surety, a childlike faith that had no room for adult doubts, dissension and despair. There was quietness in her eyes, a depth and strength such as Joe had never seen before, as if she had absorbed the things that had happened and passed into a different state of being. There was no grief, no fear, no bewilderment—just calm and acceptance and total stability. More than Glyn, more than Matthew, more than Joe himself, Ann could cope. He felt a lump come to his throat. She was too young to be independent, too young to have a baby, too young to know the meaning of life and death and love.

"Undocking—zero minus thirty minutes, and counting," said a voice across the intercom.

And Joe remembered—he was a radio operator with a job to do.

Slowly *Butterfly* edged away. Small burns from her lateral motors widened the distance between her and the *Sky Rider*. Voices marked her progress—five hundred feet, one thousand feet, increasing. Patiently Anton watched her. Twisted girders banged against her hull. But finally she was free, a winged silver shape moving against a background of fixed stars. On a new trajectory she veered away, flew on her graceful curving course toward Ganymede.

"So far so good, sir," Anton murmured.

"Any reaction from our friend?" Frobisher asked.

The pulse of light on the blueprint layout was steady now, an entity at rest among the tools and space suits in the storage closet, as if, like them, it had conducted its own check of *Butterfly* and was equally satisfied. The pattern had changed on the encephalograph. It showed the thin traces of a dormant brain, and the cardiograph registered the beat of a heart that was almost suspended.

"If I had to make a guess," said the doctor, "I would say it has gone into some form of hibernation."

It slept and was harmless, like the child.

Frobisher hoped so.

He nodded and raised his hand.

"Reverse main drive unit," Anton said crisply.

"Main drive in reverse," came the prompt reply.

"Switch on."

"We have contact."

"Maximum deceleration."

"Response maximum."

"Velocity eighteen fifty—decreasing."

"All systems go."

"She's on her way, sir," Anton said.

In the room the atmosphere relaxed. Men cheered and Frobisher smiled. It was 20:25 Earth time. Joe leaned back in his chair. He had a feeling of relief, and tiredness washed through his mind like a wave. He had been on duty for only six hours, but they were the longest hours he had ever known. He was shattered, mentally drained, as if he had given everything and had nothing left to give. It was as if he had pitched the whole of himself into *Butterfly*, his nerves wired to her computers, his voice taking control. But now she was on her way. The pressure was gone and he was returned to the vast perspectives of the control room, a man among other men and free to resume his own identity.

Blue light showed through the open doorway

of the main cabin. For the sake of the child they had readjusted the time switch, created a premature night. Secured by safety straps throughout the undocking procedure, the others lay waiting for Joe to give them permission to move, listening to the hum of the drive unit, feeling the soft vibrations in the blue dark. But Joe slipped away, went for a coffee and a wash and brush up, and when he returned ten minutes later no one answered him. The sensors showed a series of REM sleep readings.

"Leave them to sleep," the doctor advised.

"I'm not sure Frobisher will agree," Joe said.

"I'll handle Frobisher," said the doctor.

"We have an alien life form to consider."

"We have four young minds in need of rest."

"If it should make a move—"

"Then we activate the computer alarm."

"So I may as well knock off?" Joe said.

"There's no need for you to stay," the doctor agreed.

Joe nodded.

He would arrange for Hargreaves to take over the night shift, have a quick game of pool and a couple of stiff whiskeys at the Base Camp bar, and retire to his room. But Mackenzie had returned from his joyride to Jupiter and the blast of Frobisher's voice canceled Joe's plans.

"My office, Mackenzie!" Frobisher roared.

"Now! Immediately! And all senior operators to the conference room, please."

"Damn!" said Joe.

And Mackenzie cast a lingering look at the video screens.

Winged silver, a life ship flashed among the stars.

"Oh boy!" Mackenzie said. "Whose baby is that?"

15

It was minds against mechanics, a balance between psychological and scientific survival. In the small conference room Joe listened as Frobisher, Anton and the doctor hammered it out. Basalt and stars—his attention wandered. Dark beyond the window, below the lurid light of Jupiter, the surface of Ganymede stretched away, the icy landing strip where the survey ships squatted like three-legged beetles, grotesque and ugly. They talked of landing *Butterfly* out there.

"It can't be done!" Anton insisted.

"She's designed to land under vacuum conditions, isn't she?"

"Sure," said Anton. "She's a life ferry, designed to cover all eventualities. But first and foremost she's a glide lander. She utilizes atmospheric drag—that's what the parachutes are for. We don't have an atmosphere on Ganymede."

"So we use the main boosters," Frobisher said.

"She's going too fast, I tell you!"

"Plus the main drive deceleration . . ."

"I've got the initial computer report in front of me," Anton said. "There's no way we can slow her enough to ensure a safe landing."

"So you suggest we head her back to Earth?"

"We've got no choice."

Frobisher looked grim.

He knew what choice they had.

He also knew what Anton had forgotten.

"The International Federation of Spaceports will not agree to an Earth landing with an alien life form on board," Frobisher said.

Anton sat back in his chair.

His face set.

"In that case they'll have to dock at the orbiting space station."

"Pending official clearance," said Frobisher.

"Which could take months," said Joe.

"Those kids are not psychologically geared for a flight back to Earth anyway," the doctor objected. "If you do that then you're imposing

164

a prolonged stress situation which, in my opinion, they're not capable of handling. Nor am I willing to agree to drug-induced suspended animation with no direct medical supervision on board."

"So what *are* we going to do?" Anton asked.

Frobisher raised his head.

Strangely quiet at the other end of the table Mackenzie had been sitting, subdued by his earlier reprimand and not daring to speak. He had been wondering for an hour or more just why he was there. The fate of the life ferry seemed to have nothing to do with him, although more than once he had wished it did. Fast and maneuverable, she was something he would have given anything to pilot. She defied both age and time. Between heartbeat and heartbeat her warp drive engines could take her streaking away between galaxies and stars. She could travel years in the blink of an eye, and planets bloomed for her like flowers. She matched her name—a butterfly in space. Anton had no idea of her power and no idea how to handle her. With a little imagination she could be landed anywhere. Maybe Frobisher knew that. His cold eyes fixed on the younger man and seemed to read his thoughts.

"What are we going to do, Mackenzie?" Frobisher asked.

Mackenzie's heart beat faster.

He knew exactly what to do.

"Ever tried skimming a stone across a pond?" Mackenzie asked.

They stared at him, not understanding.

"It bounces," he said. "And each bounce slows it down until finally it sinks."

"Just what are you suggesting, young man?" Frobisher said.

Mackenzie nodded toward the window.

Clouds swirled with their violent colors.

Jupiter filled the sky.

"There's your pond, daddy-o," Mackenzie said. "Three hundred thousand miles of atmospheric drag. Try skimming it across that."

It was an insane plan. Yet somehow Anton knew it would work. It was not only feasible, it was calculable. Throughout the night he worked to prove it, and by 0700 hours he had the report on Frobisher's desk. They met again in the conference room at 0900 hours, although the doctor was called away for an emergency appendectomy. The initial computations, Anton said, showed that the margin for error was not unrealistically small and the consequential reduction in speed would enable *Butterfly* to land with no further problems.

"Touchdown approximately thirty-six hours from now," Anton said.

"Child's play," Mackenzie said confidently.

"I'm glad you think so," Frobisher remarked.

"There's no fail-safe, of course."

There was not only no fail-safe, no pilot on board to take over if anything went wrong with the computer schedule—there was also an alien being on board. It was that, above all else, that Frobisher feared the most. It was an unknown factor, inestimable and maybe dangerous. Neither he nor Mackenzie nor anyone else could begin to guess its potential, its power, its final intention. "It was trying to help," the girl had said—and Joe reminded him.

"You believe her?" Frobisher asked him.

"As yet I've had no reason not to believe her," Joe said.

"So you suggest we accept it as nonmalevolent?"

"I didn't say that."

"No," said Frobisher. "None of us can say that."

"Why don't we just forget about it then, daddy-o?" Mackenzie asked.

"My son," Frobisher said heavily, "there's nothing I would like better. But unfortunately I'm the Base Controller."

"There's nothing we can do about it anyway, sir," Mackenzie said.

"He's right about that," said Anton.

Frobisher sat back in his chair.

Mackenzie was not right.

"We could attempt to destroy it," Frobisher said.

It was a living thing. It might be drawn to scenes of death and disaster, but they had no proof it killed and was the cause. Joe's fist came down hard on the tabletop with an emphatic "No!" He might condone the death of disease viruses, the death of animals for food, the death of homicidal maniacs, deformed babies and terminally ill people—but he would not condone the death of a thinking, living entity simply because it was there.

"I ask you only to consider it," Frobisher said.

It was 1030 hours when Joe returned to radio control. There were no problems, Hargreaves told him. Ann and Benjamin played on the control cabin floor. Bells on a baby rattle made a soft jingle of sound. Matthew was making a meal. Caroline and Sonja still slept. And Glyn sat in one of the silver chairs wearing only his trousers.

"Not dressed yet?" Joe said.

"Where've *you* been?" Glyn asked him.

"Talking to Frobisher."

"About us?"

"What else would I be talking to him about?"

"So what's been decided?"

"You touch down in about thirty-six hours."

168

Glyn frowned.

The conception of time eluded him. Big as a football Jupiter had grown in the night, and he had only Ann's word it was morning.

"When's that?" Glyn asked.

"Late tomorrow evening," Joe said.

"You mean we've got two whole days to kill?"

"I'm afraid so."

"In that case," said Glyn, "I may as well go back to bed."

Joe watched him go—into a doorway of blue light.

Two days to kill.

It was an unfortunate choice of expression. They had two days to kill—or fail to kill an alien being and risk its revenge. Consider it, Frobisher had said. It was an old instinct. Animals killed to protect their young but men had other reasons. This was more than a protective act. It was fear of the unknown, the urge to destroy what they could not control, the elimination of an unpredictable element. The baby laughed, clutched the rattle and banged it on the floor. The bells tinkled and prickles of gold seemed to dance in the cabin light, static electric making a shimmering halo around Ann's hair. She was staring at him—her blue eyes fixed on his face in an unnerving stare.

"You shouldn't think about death and killing," Ann said softly. "That would be foolish. It can't go against what it is and neither can you. All you can do is destroy what's in yourself."

Joe leaned forward.

He sensed he was on the edge of something.

"And what exactly is it?" Joe asked her.

"Fail-safe," Ann said.

"Pardon?"

She closed her eyes. She seemed to be struggling inside her head, as if she tried to catch at a thought that was slipping away. In the gold drifting light and the sound of bells Joe waited.

"Tell me."

"Fail-safe," Ann repeated. "Fail-safe. . . . It's the only one we have." She shook her head and looked at him. "I don't know what it means," she said.

Joe knew.

Mackenzie had talked of it and he must let Frobisher know what Ann had said. But Frobisher knew already. It was red alert in the room on Ganymede.

The machines had shown a huge burst of alien activity and a surge of power. But all Joe had seen were Ann's eyes and the light that danced on her hair, and all he had heard were the rattle of baby bells and the strange ring of her words. Over and over Frobisher replayed the scene on the video screen. Vision and sound stayed the same. Nothing was added, no alien being standing beside her, no inhuman form that merged with her own, nothing visible or audible to account for the heartbeats and brainwaves that had showed on the sensors twinned for a few seconds with hers.

Invisible, immaterial, in front of their eyes, the thing had come, delivered its message and gone. Nothing remained, only Ann's unfaltering voice, captured on tape and containing its warning.

"You shouldn't think about death and killing."

"Turn it off," Frobisher said.

The replay screen went blank.

"Where is it now?" Frobisher asked.

On the blueprint layout a pulse of light showed its hiding place. It had gone to ground, coiled like a snake behind the computer casing. It had answered threat with counterthreat, the menace of its presence among the delicate microchip circuits where the breath and life and functioning of *Butterfly* ended and began. Frobisher could not touch it there.

"What now, daddy-o?" Mackenzie asked.

"We do like she says," Frobisher said grimly.

There was nothing but time—grueling hours of working and waiting, snatched meals and changing shifts, a relentless concentration of minds and mathematics, precise calculations of speeds within seconds, trajectory curves, flight paths, relative velocities, compiling details of the computer schedule, checking and confirming. The control room hummed like a beehive, a ceaseless buzzing of sound, a flurry of movements amid the light. Mackenzie droned his way through strings of figures and Frobisher came and went, his waspish tones coordinating a dozen separate procedures into one complete operation. It all had little to do with Joe.

He dealt with kids, not calculations. And for them time was even longer. Triggered by the computer, the blue dreamy light in the main cabin blazed suddenly white and there were still two whole days to go before they landed on Ganymede. Glyn buttoned his shirt. They had to re-establish a normal diurnal rhythm, a natural pattern of waking and eating and sleeping which only Benjamin had retained. "Wash," said Matthew. "Smarten yourselves up. Get something to eat and report to the main cabin." Then he woke Caroline. Drugged tired, bad-tempered and irritable. Glyn heard her screaming in the washroom. And Sonja was in an evil mood. Someone had spilled a cup of vitamin orange all over the top of her suitcase, and the communal comb was missing.

"Don't look at me!" Glyn said.

"I wouldn't want to," Sonja said sourly. "It's obvious you haven't used a comb for weeks."

It set the mood for the day. In the dragged-out hours they had nothing to do but quarrel. There was no order on board, no cooperation, no loyalty and no leadership—just Joe on the video screen trying to maintain a semblance of civilized behavior. He began to feel like judge and jury, referee, diplomat, ombudsman and Dutch uncle all rolled into one. They wore him down—Sonja's voice querulous and spiteful, goading Glyn to retaliate, Matthew shouting at them to stop it and Caroline screaming and whimpering and demanding attention. Only Ann stayed apart from it all, retained her calm—her blue eyes calm and watching, her voice steady and quiet, creating a world of her own for herself and the baby. By late afternoon Joe was sick of it—sick of their endless complaints, the succession of petty problems, their backbiting, bickering and bellyaching, the unrelieved boredom. His head ached. His nerves were on edge and his patience was wearing thin. Sooner or later he knew he would snap. Just go make a meal, he told them. But even a simple instruction turned into a major issue.

"Where's mine?" Sonja said.

"What d'you mean?" Glyn asked her.

"I notice you've brought Ann some soup—so where's mine?"

"Fetch it yourself!" Glyn told her. "She's got the baby. I'm not waiting on you—you jumped-up cowing snob!"

"Tell him, Joe!" Sonja said furiously. "He can't speak to me like that!"

Joe told them. His voice cut through the cabin like a whiplash.

"What do you think I am?" Joe asked them. "A kindergarten teacher? You're worse than a couple of two-year-olds! If you think I'm sitting here for another twenty-nine hours listening to your juvenile squabbling you've got another think coming! I've had you up to here!" He touched his neck. "You carry on, if that's what you want—but I'm leaving!"

He pushed back his chair.

The video screen went blank.

They heard background sounds from the room on Ganymede.

"Congratulations," Matthew told Sonja.

"He doesn't mean it, does he?"

"If he does you can hardly blame him."

"It's your fault!" Sonja said bitterly to Glyn.

"It was your great mouth more likely!" Glyn said.

"Why don't you both shut it!" Matthew snapped.

"Why's Joe gone, Mattoo?" Caroline asked.

"Because he can't stand us any longer," Matthew said. "And neither can I!"

Taking Caroline by the hand Matthew went into the main cabin. And Sonja stood staring at the video screen, waiting for Joe.

"I'm sorry, Joe!" Sonja said loudly.

"It's a bit late for that," Ann said quietly.

"What do you know!" Sonja said viciously.

"A damn sight more than you!" Glyn told her.

Ann bent her head. Down on the floor Benjamin shuffled, played with the laces on her shoes. And beyond the window the planet was ahead of them, growing massive in size, a thing of terror slowly swallowing the sky. Io, Callisto, Europa and Ganymede—they could identify the major moons that revolved around it. They could even pick out the features on Ganymede's surface—dark cracks and craters and bright smooth areas of ice. On that dwarfed world, beside the domed buildings where Joe worked, they were scheduled to land in less than thirty hours. Roast turkey and ice cream, Caroline had said. But Joe had abandoned them.

"Leave them to sweat!" Joe said.

And Frobisher agreed.

When Sonja called no one answered.

"What'll we do?" Sonja said desperately.

Ann picked up the baby, kissed his face.

"Isn't it obvious?" Ann asked.

16

It was obvious. Without Joe they had to learn to live together. And that was all right for some, Sonja thought bitterly. Ann and Matthew, Caroline and the baby, seemed to belong together— but she had no one. Seating for two hundred persons, the notice said, but the ship contained an unbearable emptiness and Glyn refused to speak to her. Quiet and brooding, he sat on his own at the far end of the cabin. Sonja collected her things. She would take a shower and wash her hair ready for tomorrow's landing. The towels were damp and Benjamin's baby shampoo was almost used up, but it was better than staying with *them.* The washroom door closed behind her and shut out the sight of them.

Glyn too was alone. Ann had gone with Matthew into a world where he was not, a world of children where Caroline danced in a floral nightgown and the baby ate pap from a spoon. They worked like a team, Ann and Matthew, relaxed and easy with no one to hinder them. Their words were warm and their smiles were bright, and when Benjamin was changed they all sang nursery rhymes together. A girl with a baby—Glyn could pick out Ann's voice, shy at first but growing stronger. It was sweet and clear as the Devon moors where she used to walk, and wild as the sea. Light, bright as sunshine, played on her hair, and her blue summer eyes were looking at Matthew, not him. What he witnessed was a kind of happiness that excluded him.

Glyn bit his lip. It was not jealousy he felt, but shame. He was ashamed of himself, for the way he was and the way he had acted, morose and aggressive. In the unforgiving end of the day he realized he had not only helped drive Joe away, he had driven Ann and Matthew away too. Angry and hostile and full of himself, he had not stopped to think. It did not take much to make life beautiful—just a please or a thank you, a smile for a child or the touch of a hand, just a word or a look or a gesture, a little less selfishness and a little more self-control. Ann was right. It was obvious. And the least he could do was try.

He walked down the gangway toward her.

"Can I sit by you, girlie?" Glyn asked.

And when Sonja came out of the washroom it was obvious to her too—something was going on, and it was more than a silly game of I Spy. They had been planning something. She saw it on their faces—a quick exchange of glances, a furtive smile, silent messages being passed between them. Even Caroline was involved. But when Sonja demanded to be told, they pretended not to know what she was talking about. She grew more and more angry.

"You've got no right to plot things behind my back!"

"You're getting paranoid," Glyn told her.

"There's nothing going on," Matthew insisted.

"We's being nice," Caroline explained.

"You're not obliged to join us if you don't want to," Ann said.

Sonja had no intention of obliging Ann. She trimmed her toenails and ignored them all. And they ignored her too, even Glyn. And later, when the blue dark filled the cabin and she lay isolated and apart, she heard them whispering together and heard them laugh. A huge misery welled up inside her. They liked each other and left her out. It was a kind of punishment. Bitter and lonely, she left her couch and padded through to the control cabin. The blank video screen confronted her. She sat in one of the silver chairs and gently touched the smooth cold surface. Two slow tears trickled down her face.

"Joe?" Sonja whispered. "Joe? Are you listening? Don't leave me. I've said I'm sorry. Please come back."

Sonja slept with her head in her arms and her arms resting on the computer. In the main cabin Benjamin woke like a siren at 8:15, but she continued to sleep until Joe's voice roused her. She turned her head. Sunrise filled the cabin, dawn beyond the windows, the sailor's warning, making a fiery light on the metal surfaces, touching her hands with a rosy glow. And his face was next to her on the video screen, so close she could have kissed him.

"Oh Joe!" Sonja said gladly. "You've come back!"

"It's nine thirty-five," Joe said brusquely.

"I wanted to tell you . . . to apologize . . . about yesterday . . ."

"It doesn't matter."

"It was my fault."

"Just forget about it," Joe said kindly.

"You don't hate me, do you?" Sonja said anxiously.

"Of course I don't hate you," Joe confirmed.

179

It was the start of a new day.

Sonja smiled and sat up.

It was not sunrise she saw. It was Jupiter—a revolving hell of fury and color, gigantic and dangerous. Belting cloud banks swirled and whirled, twisted and shifted, fabulous and terrifying. It was coming to meet her, gobbling colors of dust and rust, ochre and umber, vermillion and pink, whirlpools of white with hints of blue at their edges. And the lightning flashed, forked yellow charges among the gold drifting veils of light that shimmered above its atmosphere. Appalling and hideous, it came rolling toward her and she thought she would die of her own smallness, an insignificant human speck shrinking away into nothing. Dark terror showed in her eyes. Joe knew how she felt.

"It won't hurt you, sweetheart."

"It's terrible! Horrible!" Sonja said. "How can you stand living on Ganymede with that hanging over you?"

"You get used to it," Joe told her.

Glyn stuck his head through the doorway. "Awake are you?"

"Go away," Sonja told him.

"It's a beautiful day," said Glyn. "Hi, Joe."

"I want to talk to you lot," Joe said.

He saw immediately how much they had changed. Quiet and immaculate, they filed into

180

the control cabin and stood before him. Nothing remained of yesterday—no hate, no anger, no violence brooding below the surface about to erupt. Even Caroline seemed different, placid and obedient, holding Matthew's hand. Only Sonja was unaffected.

"We left you some breakfast," Glyn told her.

"Peaches," said Caroline. "Yum yum."

"And the soup's still hot," said Ann.

"Stuff it!" said Sonja.

"Don't you want any?" Matthew asked.

"I know what you're doing!" Sonja snapped. "You're just trying to get rid of me!"

No one argued with her. They just glanced at each other and smiled pityingly. It was all against one, and Sonja stood alone. Cold war, a psychological negation of all her nastiness, where kindness was cruelty and used like a weapon against her. Joe studied their faces. Someone had taken control on board *Butterfly*, restored a harmony of living and an emotional stability that the doctor had declared was impossible. Either Ann, or Matthew, or Glyn—Joe could not decide which.

"Have you seen what's outside?" Joe asked.

"Jubitoo," Caroline said promptly.

Benjamin gurgled, reached out his hands toward it.

He wanted to hold it—colors and clouds.

"Take a good look at it," Joe said.

"Why?" said Glyn.

"Because you're going down there."

"What?"

"We have to use Jupiter's atmospheric drag to slow you down."

Their faces grew pale in the light. Each pair of eyes reflected the thoughts and feelings behind them—Glyn's gray and wild, Sonja's brown and afraid, Matthew's confused behind his glasses. One by one Joe studied them, expressions of horror, and panic, and disbelief—and a slip of a girl with bone-china skin whose blue serene eyes stared into his own and controlled everything. Ann held the baby in her arms as the panic broke in the cabin around her.

"You can't send us down there!" Glyn said wildly.

"He wouldn't send us if it wasn't all right," Ann said firmly.

It was hard to define how she did it, but her words took command and they turned toward her, as if she were the only one who knew what was happening, the only one who could tell them. In the shifting patterns of fiery light, where the drive units hummed like music and the strands of her hair moved pale and golden in the currents of warm air, she stood alone and told them what

182

they needed to hear. Simple and logical, she seemed to touch them with her own quietness, instill in them the same unquestionable trust. It was almost magical.

Joe was impressed.

"How long have we got?" Glyn asked him.

"Eight hours," Joe said.

He could feel the tension in the cabin as he outlined their plan. He could feel the fear that Ann controlled but could not dispel. And he could feel the pressure building up in the room beyond him, men and computers, checking and finalizing as the time slipped away. He was the link between them—between Ganymede and *Butterfly*—between the quiet routine of the ship and the gathering chaos of countdown.

"We need a fail-safe," Joe said.

"What's that?" said Glyn.

Joe explained.

"You mean we've got to learn to pilot this thing ourselves?"

"Not quite," said Joe. "You'll be computer controlled."

"Then what's the point?"

"It's just a precautionary measure."

"In case of what?"

"In case something should go wrong," Matthew said.

"Or in case we lose contact," said Joe.

"Is that likely?" Sonja asked in alarm.

It was extremely unlikely.

But they had to make allowances.

"Don't worry," Joe said lightly. "It may never happen."

It might never happen, but Sonja had nothing else to do but think of it. Along with Ann and Caroline and Benjamin she was sent from the control cabin while Glyn and Matthew took training, and an American pilot called Mackenzie took over the radio from Joe. He was young and extroverted and his talk was crazy. For a while Sonja watched him from the doorway, but he was not interested in her—he cared only about *Butterfly*. They could fly her with their eyes shut, he told Glyn and Matthew. There was nothing to it. Nothing but dials and switches and instrument readings, speed tracers, velocity differentials, altimeters, vector burns, computer checks, main drive acceleration and all systems copy. Nothing but a manual takeover procedure they would never need to initiate. It was all very boring. It was even more boring than being with Ann and Caroline. Sonja wandered away.

And after lunch it was the same—herself and Ann in the walled-in main cabin with the silver glitter of seats and Caroline growing touchy, time getting later and later as Mackenzie's voice drawled on. They were like separate people, no longer knowing each other and no Joe to bind them together. Caroline dumped Uggy on Sonja's lap.

"I don't want the damned thing!" Sonja said. "It stinks!"

Matthew heard the voices shouting.

Words and distractions.

Caroline and Sonja.

"Concentrate!" Mackenzie told him.

They began again.

Theoretical actions in a game of let's pretend.

His head ached.

"Fail contact—situation critical."

"Commence manual takeover."

The same words.

The same procedure.

Repeated and repeated.

The American voice drove him.

"Take it again. She's your baby."

"Stop pestering me!" Sonja shouted.

Caroline screamed.

There was nothing Matthew could do.

Glyn and Mackenzie bound him to stay.

"Fail contact—situation critical."

The ship crossed the orbit of Ganymede in midafternoon. There was no sky, no stars—just the planet ahead of them, the colors revolving— ochre, umber, blue and vermillion. It was all

185

swirling and shifting, light on the instruments, colors in the cabin around him. His responses faltered. His eyes played tricks on him and the headache grew worse. But still Mackenzie's drawling voice went on.

"Fail contact—situation critical."

"Height seventeen fifty miles," said Glyn. "And falling."

"Velocity," said Matthew. "Velocity—forty-five miles per second and falling."

"How do you know?" Mackenzie asked him.

"By checking the speed-trace reading."

"Indicate the speed tracer."

"There," said Matthew.

"You twit!" said Glyn. "That's the altimeter."

Matthew closed his eyes.

The main drive droned through his mind, relentless noise and a mass of figures. It was all falling apart. Garish colors pulsed and spun. And when he looked it was still happening—ochre and umber, blue and vermillion—shifting and drifting across a blur of dials. Harsh light glittered on chrome fittings and the video screen flickered. Mackenzie's face closed and receded, and all around the brightness flashed and throbbed with the pain in his head. Waves of sickness washed through him. His hands were clammy and cold.

"You all right, boyo?" Glyn asked him.

Zero minus 120 minutes, and counting.

Mackenzie heard the voice across the inter-'com.

And Matthew clutched his head.

"I've got a migraine," Matthew said.

"Oh boy!" Mackenzie murmured.

Frobisher was going to love that.

17

Zero minus ten minutes, and counting.

Glyn was on his own.

Matthew was sick, and *Butterfly* carried a cupboard full of drugs, but there was nothing for migraine. It would have to run its course, the doctor said, and even if there was an emergency Matthew would not be fit enough to handle the ship. He lay in the main cabin, strapped down with the rest of them on the silver couches, with a cold compress covering his eyes. And Glyn was alone with no one to help him—just Joe on Ganymede 270,000 miles away. It won't happen, Joe kept telling him, but that was no consolation.

Banks of brown cloud came hurtling toward him, a sensation of speed after stillness that made him feel sick too. Up and down resumed their true meanings. Above were the moons and stars in the blackness of space, and below were thousands of miles of wallowing atmosphere. It was great, Mackenzie had said, just like a roller coaster ride. It was all right for him, but Glyn had cramps in his stomach. His throat turned dry and his sweat was stinking of fear.

Zero minus five minutes, and counting.

"I want to go," Glyn said.

"You can't," said Joe. "There isn't time."

"If anything goes wrong . . ."

"It won't," Joe assured him.

"I can't remember none of it!"

"You won't have to."

But there was no such thing as certainty.

A pulse of light stirred on the blueprint layout.

And hurricane winds whipped up Jupiter's clouds.

"How long now?" Glyn asked.

Zero minus three minutes, and counting.

The sense of loneliness was hideous.

Glyn wanted to leave, go lie with the rest of them in the windowless cabin, without seeing or knowing. He wanted to close his eyes and stay blind to everything. But something fluttered at the corner of his vision, a movement of gold and beige among the light. He turned his head. Ann smiled briefly, came to join him in the chair beside him and fastened the safety straps.

Zero minus two minutes.

"I think you should go," Joe said quickly.

"I came to be with Glyn," Ann said.

Glyn reached for her hand and squeezed it.

She had come to be with him, but it was more than that—deeper, more instinctive, almost a compulsion. She had to stay, although she did not know why, and it was not just for Glyn's sake she had come. Something had called her deep in her mind, the strains of a song, urgent as life. Ganymede switched onto red alert.

Alien activity—the sensors showed it, brainwaves and heartbeats and a surge of power. Some formless entity, liquid and invisible, moved through the computer circuits, flowed out into the cabin and was drawn toward her, as if her voice had triggered it and her presence lured it awake. With one minute to go Frobisher made the connection.

"Get that girl out of there!" Frobisher howled.

"Go back to the main cabin!" Joe told Ann.

"No!" said Glyn. "Stay with me, girlie."

"Go quickly!" said Joe. "I haven't time to argue."

But it was too late.

190

Prickles of gold light danced and accumulated, making pale aureoles of fire around Ann's hair. Soft bell sounds filled the air, thin as gnat whines and almost inaudible amid the drone of the main drive unit. Glyn never heard them, but the sonic separator picked them up, hypnotic, subliminal, alien music affecting Ann's mind. Glazed and motionless, her blue eyes stared into nowhere and Joe could not get through to her.

"Hang on to your couches!" Glyn shouted. "Here we go!"

A misty nimbus veiled *Butterfly*'s wings, the first faint traces of atmosphere, thin as spindrift above an ocean of cloud. She dived toward it. Clean as a fish she curved and entered, her silver fins cleaving a path. On Ganymede the external scanners followed her, showed her rising and falling across the video screens as the men watched and held their breaths. She was a perfect machine, graceful and delicate, her responses smooth as a shark's. Flawless, beautiful, computer controlled—Mackenzie knew she would answer exactly to the scheduled instructions. Her speed dropped dramatically . . . 850 . . . 750 . . . 650 miles per second.

"Go, baby, go!" Mackenzie muttered.

There was nothing to go wrong with her. Everything functioned according to plan. But he saw in the cabin a human girl engulfed in a pillar of flickering light, an alien life form merging with hers, an alien intelligence taking her over—some godawful entity with its terrible power. A harbinger of disaster, someone had said. But it was not the girl or the alien that threatened *Butterfly*. It was Jupiter. Forked lightning flashed among towering cumulus, and directly ahead of them a white spot broke the surface, heaved up from the raging atmosphere beneath, a whirling hurricane a thousand miles wide.

"God almighty!" Mackenzie groaned.

"They're heading straight for it!" Anton said.

"Course correction!" Frobisher shouted. "Quickly, man!"

The clouds changed color, paled and whitened. Lightning flashed outside and the ship struck turbulence, shuddered as a boom of sound reverberated through her walls. Sonja screamed. In the buffeting winds *Butterfly* rocked and shifted, dipped and rose—a sickening motion. At any minute Glyn thought he was going to throw up. White and gold, the lightning flickered next to him in the chair where Ann sat, but he did not have time to look.

"Keep your eyes on those dials," Joe told him.

Speed 150 and falling.

Altitude 1750 and falling.

"I want you to start talking and keep on talking," Joe said.

Speed 120.

Altitude 1650.

"We're going too low!" said Glyn.

"Just hang on," said Joe. "We'll get you out of there."

His voice crackled.

Speed 100, and falling.

Altitude 1550 miles.

"Keep talking. Keep talking."

Blue electricity forked past the cabin windows. Thunder bashed against the hull. The wind sucked them down in a whirling spiral. Like a small canoe the ship was jolted in the rocking clouds. Something crashed in the main cabin and Sonja screamed again. "Keep talking! Keep talking!" Joe said. But his voice dissolved in a roar of static and his face on the video screen was gone to a pattern of wavy lines. Fail contact. Situation critical. Velocity 75 miles per second, and falling. Altitude 1450 miles, and falling. Commence manual takeover.

"Mummy! Mummy!" Caroline screamed. "I want to go home!"

Blind panic took hold of Glyn's mind.

"What'll I do? Tell me! Tell me! What'll I do?" Glyn cried.

Ann leaned forward.

She saw nothing but the aura of her own hands reaching for the switches. She heard nothing but the music in her head, a soft voice singing in some unknown language that her mind translated into actions and her muscles obeyed. She did not know what she was doing, not in words or clear thought. She only knew she must take over the ship, that only the song could save them. She switched off the radio. The static ceased and Glyn heard the wind go whistling past the windows. He heard music in the thundering sound. But he could not think of it.

Velocity 60 miles per second, and falling.

Altitude 1275 miles, and falling.

"Help me!" Glyn said.

"Manual takeover," said Ann.

"What?"

"Manual takeover. Do it! Do it!"

Mackenzie's instructions came muddling back. Glyn threw the switches to shut down the computer and the last link with Ganymede was broken. The ship headed downward. Retro burn, retro burn, some vague memory kept repeating—get her nose up. But Ann had already done it and the vectors were firing. And still the ship went down. Glyn did not stop to think about it. He slammed the main drive unit into its forward position. They had maximum acceleration. The velocity increased but the altitude continued to fall . . . 950 miles . . . 850 miles. She was caught in the spiral of the storm with not enough power to break free.

"Fire the main boosters," Ann said.

"The what?"

"The main boosters! Fire them!"

"I don't know where they are!"

Glyn glanced at her.

She was not Ann at all. She was pale and ghostly, a shimmering girl, lost in a mist of golden light. And the light danced around her, like dust motes in the sun, cells of a being that had no form but clung to her for its shape. Music touched him, lilting and beautiful, tones of a language he could not interpret, the speech of a song. It seemed to hold him, a voice within light, the eyes that were blue and deep and had once belonged to Ann. He knew no fear. He knew no sense of death or urgency. For a few split seconds it was all suspended. His mind grew empty and the knowledge entered his brain.

"Fire the main boosters," Ann repeated.

In a kind of trance Glyn turned away and reached for the controls. The main boosters fired and *Butterfly* broke free, dived and soared as the lateral thrusters steered her skyward. It was wild, glorious, a blazing trail through the massed clouds where the colors flashed past them—umber, ochre, blue and vermillion, tinting *Butterfly*'s wings. In a burst of flame from her main exhausts she veered away on a curving upward tangent and cleared the atmosphere. Jupiter fell behind. Ahead were the stars, eternally still, gold and shining in the velvet blackness of space.

It was all over. The boosters cut into silence, drained and useless. Glyn was spent like the song that faded from his mind, emptying like water out of his heart and his head. For a few seconds longer Ann retained it—hands of a girl in the dusty light setting their course in the on-board computer until she too grew still. The intensity fled from her eyes. Gold prickles danced round her hair and withdrew, dissolved with the music into the walls, or the empty air or the space outside them. The last tiny bell sound was gone. They were back with the drone of the drive units building up speed, the blank video screen, Caroline's sobs, a shut-down radio and a different fear. Pale faced, they gazed at each other.

"How do we tell them?" Glyn asked.

The men watched in horror. White clouds swallowed the ship and the contact failed. There was nothing they could do. They stood appalled by their own helplessness. All their technology was useless. Men against nature—neither they nor their machines could go against the giant planet. Luck or fate had let Mackenzie escape

196

with his life, but there was no escape for *Butterfly*. In a funnel of wind the storm sucked her down, a metal artifact, ineffectual as driftwood.

"They've had it," Mackenzie said dully.

"If they've switched through to manual . . ." Anton murmured.

"They've still had it," Mackenzie said. "That last altitude reading showed less than a thousand miles. They would need to fire the main boosters to break from a G force like that."

Minutes ticked by.

A hush filled the control cabin. Outside the base, massive and tireless, the scanners continued to pan the atmosphere, relaying their pictures of scudding cloud and revealing nothing. *Butterfly* was gone. Unwitnessed and abandoned she smashed to pieces on the frozen surface. Mackenzie covered his face with his hands. His broken voice seemed to speak for all of them.

"It was my fault!" Mackenzie said.

"We did what we could," Frobisher told him.

But it had not been enough.

Ann and Sonja, Glyn and Matthew, Caroline and the baby were dead. Joe put down the headphones. More than any man there he had grown to love them. Mackenzie might shoulder the blame for the idea that went wrong, for the genius that failed, but he was still young enough to cry. Joe was older. He had a grief that could not be expressed, not there in that room, not in public. He made for the door. Turkey roasted in the kitchen ovens. The meringue was whipped for the baked Alaska. But no little girl would sit down at the table to eat it. The music machines would stay silent. No one would dance at the party arranged for their welcome under the garlands that were hung in the main canteen. They were dead, all of them.

Joe walked through the long corridors. He did not see what Frobisher saw. He did not hear the shout of voices. With her main boosters firing, *Butterfly* rose from the clouds. She was thousands of miles away from her last point of entry but the scanners had located her—a streak of silver, beautiful and unscarred. Joy and relief showed in Mackenzie's eyes.

"She's made it, daddy-o! Oh boy! She's made it!"

Frobisher nodded.

She had made it.

But she could never land on Ganymede.

18

There had been times when Matthew thought the ship was out of control, when he thought they would crash on the surface of Jupiter and die—when Sonja screamed and Caroline clung to him in terror, and he had no way of knowing what went on. But it was over now. The noise and the buffeting had stopped. In the stillness of the light he lay and listened. Small sounds reached him out of silence—the drone of the main drive unit, Benjamin gurgling contentedly in the opposite seat, the plastic creak of Sonja's couch, Glyn and Ann talking together in the control cabin and Caroline's steady breathing. Across the last few thousand miles of space they headed toward Ganymede and a final landfall. But no one came to tell him.

"What are they doing out there?" Sonja said impatiently.

"Big bangs," Caroline said fearfully. "All big bangs, Mattoo."

"The big bangs have gone," Matthew told her.

"So what are they doing?" Sonja repeated.

There was only one way to find out.

"You stay here," Matthew told Caroline.

But it was too soon to leave her.

Her body stiffened in his arms.

"Big bangs! Big bangs!" Caroline shrilled.

"Not anymore," Matthew said. "You listen."

"You don't go! You don't go, Mattoo!"

"I'll go," said Sonja.

Streaks of tears had dried on her cheeks and her hair was a mess. Bruised and shaken, she undid the safety straps. Her legs felt like jelly and she had to hold on to the seats to help herself walk. Quiet light shone down the length of the gangway, a green distance of floor between rows of silver seats, abandoned and empty. The sensation frightened her. And when she reached the control cabin something was wrong. There was no Joe, no excitement. Just a switched-off radio and a blank video screen, Ann and Glyn leaning against the computer, impassive faces silent and watching her.

"You should have waited," Glyn told her.

"We were coming to tell you," Ann said.

Sonja knew what they would tell her.

But she had to ask.

"Where's Joe?"

"We lost contact," Glyn said.

But it was more than that. Something was wrong, and they knew it. They looked at each other and Sonja felt the panic rising.

"Where *is* he?"

"Gone," said Glyn.

"We can't get him back," Ann said.

"What do you mean?" Sonja said angrily. "Of course we can get him back! You haven't even tried! Get out of the way and I'll do it!"

She crossed the cabin to the radio.

But Glyn caught her arm.

"You can't do that, girlie," Glyn said softly.

"Let go of me!" Sonja said viciously.

"You can't touch that radio."

"We've got to get through to Joe!"

"Joe's gone, I tell you!"

"Take your hands off my arm—you Welsh oaf!"

His grip tightened.

"Listen, you! You ain't going to do nothing."

"I'll report you for this!" Sonja shrieked.

"When we get to Ganymede I'll report you!"

"We're not going to Ganymede!" Glyn shouted.

"What?" said Sonja.

Everything grew still.

Glyn released her in the frozen light.

And blue and cold was the pity in Ann's eyes.

"We're not going to Ganymede," Ann repeated. "Do you understand that?"

Matthew heard their raised voices.

Something was wrong.

And Caroline sensed it too.

"Big bangs," Caroline whimpered.

Only Benjamin remained unperturbed. Almost upended, he lay on the couch and played with his feet, a muddle of fingers and toes, moving extremities which he gazed at and talked to. Matthew fumbled to undo the harness of stocking tights and safety straps that bound him. His hands were shaking. Remnants of dull pain throbbed in his head and the light flickered at the corner of his vision—gold on silver, a combination of migraine and glasses. Something was wrong. Something was missing. Joe failed to check the anger rising and the radio was silent. Matthew lifted Benjamin free of the seat and dumped him on the floor, gave him the bell rattle that had once belonged to Eleanor. His fat fingers grasped and clutched it and the bells jingled.

"Stay and look after him," he told Caroline. Blue fear showed in her eyes.

Benjamin was her baby brother and she was responsible, but once before she had stayed to look after him. She had waited and waited and her mother never came back. Now she watched Matthew walk away and the fear was the same inside her. Tears filled her eyes and her shrill cry halted him.

"You don't go, Mattoo! You don't leave me!"

He turned and looked back. Feelings tore at him. He was caught between Glyn and Sonja, the screaming anger and a distressed little girl. Between violence and tears he was being torn in two directions at once.

"You don't leave me, Mattoo," Caroline said plaintively.

And Glyn's voice howled through his brain.

"We're not going to Ganymede!" Glyn shouted.

Everything stopped. It was as if time were frozen and the universe ended and only Benjamin continued—a baby playing with a rattle, jingling bells that were soft and sad, requiem music for every life that had ended. Pictures flashed in Matthew's mind—his mother's smile, his father's face, his sister's wedding day and Eleanor's birth, and a vision of Joe on the video screen. Emotions dragged at him. In the elements of pure sound he wanted to cry for everything he had loved and lost. The light grew blurred. Liquid and golden it shimmered and moved, dissolving Caroline in a mist of tears and taking Benjamin away.

"We're not going to Ganymede," Ann repeated. "Do you understand that?"

And the grief that began was not Matthew's.

It was a wailing hysterical crying of absolute despair.

Matthew leaned against the computer and tried to stay calm. A string of moons trailed out into space and Sonja sank to her knees, rested her head on the chair and cried. Joe was gone and they were not going to Ganymede.

"We fired the main boosters," Glyn said. "There's no power left, see? So we can't land."

"And there's nothing Joe can do to help us," Ann said.

"Have you tried asking him?" Matthew inquired.

"They won't let me," Sonja wept.

"There's no point," said Glyn.

"We can't do it," said Ann. "We can't do it—not to Joe. My dad had to tell my mother. He had to tell her she was going to die and there was nothing anyone could do. And then he had to watch her. We can't make Joe tell us, watch us. . . . It's too cruel!"

204

"So we just sit back and wait to die?" Matthew said. "Is that what you're saying?"

"No," said Ann. "No, not that. I'm not talking about death."

"Then what are you talking about?"

"It's just that he can't help us to live," Ann said.

"He can't get us out of here, see?" said Glyn.

"Only the music can do that," Ann said.

Matthew listened.

It was not just music. It was a mind, a voice, a living being that had told them what to do and saved their lives. They would have been dead on the surface of Jupiter if the music had not saved them. And now they had no choice but to trust it—trust that it would take them where they wanted to go, anywhere across the galaxy toward the stars.

"No!" Sonja cried. "You can't do that! We've got to get through to Joe. Tell them, Matthew! Tell them! They won't listen to me! We can't get back without Joe. Tell them!"

Matthew frowned.

"Back where?"

"Home!" said Sonja. "Back to Earth!"

Glyn shook his head. And slowly, in the silence, in the appeal of Ann's eyes, Matthew began to understand. They had no home back on Earth. A home was with people, but people were dead. Ann's people, Sonja's people, his own family—

all of them dead. And Glyn had left home out of choice. Their home was here, on *Butterfly*, wherever she went, and Joe could never be a part of them. For that reason alone they had to trust the music. But Sonja cried in her need and her loneliness and failed to see. Matthew squatted beside her and put an arm around her shoulder.

"We can't go back, Sonja."

"I don't understand!" Sonja sobbed.

"We can only go forward."

"There's nothing left without Joe!"

"There's us."

"You don't want me!"

"You got to give us a chance, girlie," Glyn said.

"You hate me! I know you do!"

"Are you sure it's not you who hates yourself?" Matthew asked her.

"I don't understand!"

"Isn't there anything you love?" Ann asked.

Sonja looked up.

Light reflected on the empty video screen. She loved Joe, but Joe was gone. He was gone! He was gone! And Ann smiled at her and Matthew had his arm around her shoulder and Glyn offered her his handkerchief. They expected her to like them for that. They expected her to believe what they said—believe in some fairy-tale music she had never heard, that a genie of light would appear out of nowhere and transport them away to wherever they wanted to go. They were crazy, all of them. She was surrounded by mad people—lunatic eyes, blue and gray and bespectacled, cruel kind voices murmuring insane words.

"You don't need to worry, girlie."

"You'll be all right."

"You'll be all right with us."

"We'll look after you."

"It's better this way."

"Joe can't help us, see?"

"He'll know we're alive."

"He'll know that much."

"We'll pass over Ganymede soon and their scanners will find us."

"And afterward we'll talk about it."

"We'll talk about where we're going."

"If you really want to go back to Earth . . ."

"Stop it!" said Sonja. "Stop it! Stop it!"

"You have a good cry," Glyn told her.

"It'll make you feel better," Ann said gently.

"We're sorry about Joe."

"We *are* sorry."

Sonja leaned her head against Matthew's shoulder.

And their voices went on, breaking her down, battering her mind.

"Tell them to stop it," Sonja wept.

But it was Caroline who stopped it.

"Butt'flies! Butt'flies!" Caroline shrilled. She came running into the cabin. Her face was flushed and her eyes were bright with excitement. "Butt'flies! Butt'flies! You come!"

"Where?" said Matthew.

"In there! In there!" Caroline babbled. "Lots of butt'flies. You come and see, Mattoo. Quick! Quick!"

"What's she talking about?" Glyn asked. He went to the doorway.

"Oh glory," Glyn murmured. "Come and look."

"You come, Sonja," Caroline said.

Ann and Matthew helped her to her feet.

It was a vision Sonja saw. The cabin was alive with butterflies, yellow wings fluttering above the seats, hatching from the air vents and gathering together in a haze of golden light.

And in the midst of the light a boy was standing, not formed out of flesh and blood as they were, but made of the light itself, a being shimmering and insubstantial. He was watching the butterflies that fluttered around his head. His laughter was music and Benjamin sat at his feet, jigged and gurgled and raised his fat baby hands toward him. Sonja held her breath. He was the magic Ann had talked of. He was the power that would take them traveling across the universe to another home. Words of a song went echoing through her mind.

> *With me there's no loneliness, lady—*
> *just endless flight—*
> *metal angels on the star roads—*
> *wings among the light.*

Ann squeezed her hand.

"If only Joe could see him," Sonja said.

Joe stood by the observatory window. Ahead of him, beyond the horizon, Jupiter filled the sky, but he saw no beauty in it. It was a terrible, violent place. The clouds swirled, shedding a lurid light along the icy landing strip, staining the scanners with colors of rust and blood. Spots, white as leprosy, burst and spread in the ulcerous atmosphere. Once he had loved it, thrilled to its power. Veiled and mysterious, it drew him like a challenge. But now he saw it for what it was—a gigantic world, treacherous and dangerous, raging elements that indiscriminately destroyed and made people ineffectual against them. Born on a tamed Earth, people were apt to forget—it did not take much to redress the balance, just a human error or a mechanical breakdown, just the forces of nature and a few seconds of time.

"Better than a roller coaster ride," Mackenzie had said.

And six children had died.

For a long time Joe stood there staring from the windows. Small as a marble, Europa passed along its orbit, casting a moony shadow on Jupiter's clouds. And something flashed silver beside it, tiny as a speck of sunlight on an insect's wing. Joe narrowed his eyes—but it dipped below the line of craters and was gone. The streak of a meteorite, Joe thought, and minds clutched at anything to stave off the grief. Hope flickered and died. He did not hear the person coming behind him, the soft tread of shoes on the linoleum floor. He did not know he was not alone until Frobisher spoke to him.

"I thought I would find you here," Frobisher said.

"I needed to be alone," Joe said grimly.

"They're not dead, you know," Frobisher told him.

Joe stared at him.

He could not believe it at first.

They were not dead, Frobisher told him, not crashed on the surface of Jupiter. They had fired the main boosters and escaped from the gravitational pull. But with the boosters drained of power they could not land on Ganymede. Recharge was automatic but it would take several weeks, and on their present trajectory they would be clear of the solar system before that happened.

They were heading outward, Frobisher said, accelerating toward the stars. And they had made no effort to reestablish contact. He assumed they were being controlled.

"Better if they had died," Joe said bitterly.

"For them maybe," Frobisher admitted. "But not for us."

"Is there nothing we can do?"

"I'm afraid not, Joe."

"We just wash our hands and absolve ourselves of the blame?"

"If they will let us," Frobisher said quietly.

He turned to stare from the windows, as if he were watching for something. Motionless beside the hangars, the survey ships squatted and the massive scanners slowly panned the far horizon. Straight and clean the runway stretched toward it, a man-made scar softened by Jupiter's flickering colors. And suddenly, along its length and on either side of it, the lights switched on—electric yellow in a blaze of welcome for a ship that could not land.

"She should pass over us any minute now," Frobisher said.

Joe clenched his fists.

Some alien inhuman thing had hold of *Butterfly* and staged a fly past, as if to honor them—the conquered or the dead. The irony cut like a pain. And she shot like a bullet over the rim of the craters, flew fast and low toward the buildings. The speed of her, the size of her, the absolute perfect control was terrifying to watch. In a streak of silver, where the walls shuddered and the floors vibrated, she lifted and was gone, over and above them faster than eyes could follow. Joe went to cross the room and watch from the opposite windows, but Frobisher caught his arm.

"What's that?" Frobisher said.

Against a background of black sky, on the far side of the observatory, prickles of gold light danced in the empty air, shimmered and gathered into a sphere that whirled and spun. Joe could hear music, tiny bell-like sounds. He watched as the light lengthened to a pillar of flame—gold fire and someone standing there. Just for a moment Joe saw him, a boy among mist. And just for a moment he heard him speak, a language of music he could not understand. Then the flame shrank, became a sphere again, disintegrated and was gone. The bell sounds faded, leaving only an echo in his head, a quiet memory, a feeling of peace and thankfulness and trust.

"What was it?" said Frobisher. "A vision or something?"

Joe knew.

It was something more than a vision. It had left behind it some tangible evidence, a pale shape that moved and fluttered, beating its wings against the window glass—a solitary butterfly. Joe approached it, touched it gently, a quivering living thing, sulfurous and dusty.

"*Gonepteryx rhamni,*" Joe said.

"What?" said Frobisher.

"A yellow brimstone."

And beyond it, small as a pinprick, its namesake was speeding away, a silver cocoon with its precious cargo of life. Ann and Sonja, Glyn and Matthew, Caroline and the baby—he had known them and loved them and now he watched them go. They went with a golden boy into the future toward an unknown star. He knew they would make it.

"Good-bye, *Butterfly,*" Joe said softly.

About the Author

LOUISE LAWRENCE was born in Surrey, England, and now lives in Gloucestershire. Ms. Lawrence has been writing since she was twenty-two, and has since published eight novels for young adults. Her books CHILDREN OF THE DUST and CALLING B FOR BUTTERFLY were both ALA Best Books for Young Adults.